Why don't people want to talk about Laurie?

All anyone has to do is say 'Laurie Jenkins' and everybody goes to pieces. Strong boys disappear, kids in assembly get in an argument, Penn's face goes blank, Stephen and Tessa knock things over. She must be one intense girl! I wonder if she was as interesting when she was around as she is now that she's gone.

Am I jealous? Maybe. I get sick of hearing Laurie's name, and yet in spite of myself I sometimes feel I want to know all about her. In that slide of the car wash she looks so ordinary. I wouldn't have guessed that her running away would leave such a hole in so many lives. Sometimes when her name comes up, it's as if a cold breath is blowing on the back of my neck and I have the eerie feeling that something is wrong. Why don't people want to talk about Laurie? What's going on? Where did she go?

D0469278

Don't miss the other books in this exciting series,

THE
SECRET
Diaries

THE
SECRET
Diaries

VOLUME I
TEMPTATION

JANICE HARRELL

SCHOLASTIC INC.
New York Toronto London Auckland Sydney

ISBN 0-590-47692-0

Copyright © 1994 by Daniel Weiss Associates, Inc., and Janice Harrell. All rights reserved. Published by Scholastic Inc.

Produced by Daniel Weiss Associates, Inc.
33 West 17th Street, New York, NY 10011

12 11 10 9 8 7 6 5 4 3 2 1   4 5 6 7 8/9

Printed in the U.S.A.   01

First Scholastic printing, May 1994

TEMPTATION

One

Dear Diary,

I'm not sure I want to write this down, Diary, not even in our secret language. Someone else would probably think it's weird that I write my diary entries in code. But now that I have so much to hide, it's a good thing I developed the habit. I wish I could just close my eyes and go to sleep and pretend none of it happened.

But I have to tell someone. And who else can I tell? It's not as if I have a million best friends dying to hear all my secrets. Dying. Great word choice, Joanna.

At least I know my secret will be safe with you. Though you wouldn't think safety was a big concern of mine. Not after I got involved in such terrible things.

It all started on my first day at Barton High. . . .

"No joke! Molly and Jeff were having sex in Jeff's Geo," said an earnest girl in a red ski jacket.

"Impossible," argued her freckle-faced friend. "A Geo is way too little. There'd be arms and legs sticking out all the windows."

"Would you quit interrupting? The point is, a policeman turned his spotlight right in the car."

A breeze blowing across the school sidewalk made them all shiver.

"How embarrassing!" A small girl with a froggy voice thrust her pockets deep into her jacket.

"Humiliating is more like it. And that's not the worst part!" said the girl in the red ski jacket. "He made them show their driver's licenses and then he said he was going to have to notify Molly's parents because she was underage!"

"There are a lot of sadists in the police force," put in the freckled girl.

"So what happened?" the frog-voiced girl asked.

The girl in the ski jacket shrugged. "Nothing. A call came in on the cop's radio and all of a sudden he left. I guess he had to go chase criminals."

I realized that these girls were so busy gossiping that they were never going to notice I was standing there waiting to ask my simple question. All I needed to know was how to get to my physics class. It was no big deal, but I didn't want to begin my first day at this new school by being late. I cleared my throat, but the frog-voiced girl still didn't notice me. "The problem is," she said, "that police are poking around all over the place ever since—"

"Hey, do you need help?" the girl in the red ski jacket asked me suddenly. They all turned to look at me.

"Could you tell me which building is Eastman?" I asked, flushing.

"I'll take you there," said the frog-voiced girl. "I'm going in that direction."

"Thanks."

"You new?"

I nodded.

"Your dad get transferred into town or something?" She eyed me curiously as we walked.

The last thing I wanted to do was to go into the details of what had brought me to Barton City, North Carolina. "I've just come to live with my dad," I said.

"My parents are divorced, too," the girl confessed. "Awful, isn't it? That's Eastman, right over there."

The brick walls of Eastman were drenched with the morning sunlight. The long building extended out onto a slope and was two stories tall at its far end. A couple of guys were sitting on the brick wall next to the steps, legs dangling. One had turned his face to the sky. He was an ash blond and was wearing a white shirt, sleeves rolled up to the elbows and open at the throat. He was too far away for me to see his face clearly, but he had leaned an arm against a pillar and he seemed to be stretching, uncoiling with the easy grace of a cat. I couldn't remember ever seeing anyone look so relaxed. Several other kids were with him, but I could only see that one boy.

"Don't get your hopes up," said my guide, seeing me transfixed.

"Maybe I could get to know them." I was hardly aware that I was speaking. I was thinking out loud.

My companion made a face. "I'll give you a little tip. That group isn't one of the friendliest."

When I glanced at her in surprise, she was gazing at the kids by the railing with a look I couldn't quite decipher. Envy? Pity?

"Besides," she began, then stopped and lowered her eyes.

"Besides *what?*" I insisted. "Is there something about them I should know?"

"Something you should know?" she repeated. "No, not really. It's just they're a very tight clique. Look, I don't want you to get the wrong impression of the school. Forget I said anything, okay?"

"Who's the blond guy?" I asked. As if a string were stretched between us, I was drawn to him. He looked good, but that wasn't all that attracted me. I think it was something about the way he moved—as if he had all the time and all the self-confidence in the world. I was confused, and he seemed so on top of things.

"That's Penn Parrish," she said shortly. "Interested?"

I shrugged noncommittally.

"Well, it's a waste of energy." She snorted. "You aren't his type. Besides, those guys aren't what you'd think just by looking at them."

"Oh, really?" I said encouragingly.

"I've got a big mouth." She grinned. "And, hey, I'd better watch out or you're going to be late to class. Take my advice—this is a friendly school, but you've got to make the effort. What you should do is join a lot of clubs right off. It's the best way to get to know people. You only get out of it what you put in. I'm Nikki Warren, by the way."

"I'm Joanna Rigsby," I said.

"Look, Joanie, if I can help you out or anything, just give me a call, okay? No kidding."

"Joanna," I corrected her automatically, but I was speaking to empty air. She had turned and vanished without even giving me her phone number.

A friendly school.

Right, I thought. The idea of having to sing in some geeky glee club in order to get to know people depressed me beyond words.

I wanted to turn around right that minute and walk back to my car and drive away, but the impulse didn't last. What kept me there, looking down as if I were trying to find deeper meaning in the torn cellophane wrappers and the bent cigarette butts ground into the scraggly grass, was that I was remembering all too vividly what I had escaped by coming here.

This was my third school since my parents' divorce. My most recent had been Covenant Day School. I had hated the teachers there, with their weak grasp of their subjects and their belief that earthly things didn't matter to those who love the Lord. Also the dress code was a serious problem.

My blond hair is long, and looks best with dangling earrings, which were strictly forbidden at Covenant. The uniforms were made of stiff itchy gray flannel and constantly smelled of mothballs.

Still, I probably could have put up with the school until I graduated in the spring. Unfortunately, my mother had gotten so eccentric, so scary, that I had to put in a distress call to my father.

I came to live with my father only days before Christmas break was to end. And when I looked around at Barton High that first time—the sturdy brick buildings, the sunlight glancing off wide, modern windows, kids racing by in ripped jeans and high-top sneakers, and Penn Parrish balancing on the wall—it seemed like the most normal sort of school. I hoped I could find a place for myself here. But I couldn't help feeling tense. A cold breeze brushed me like a premonition of danger.

Two

Well, my first day at Barton High could
have been worse. Sure, the only person who
spoke to me sounded like a frog, but it's got
to get better from here—right?

I can't stop thinking about that guy
Penn. Okay, I know, it's crazy—I don't even
know him. But I wonder what his voice
sounds like? I wonder what he eats for
breakfast? I wonder how I can meet him?

I did my best to settle into my new school,
but it wasn't easy. Because of a severe locker
shortage, I had to share with a girl whose ratty
black hair cascaded from a topknot on her head.
Her face was white—she really laid on the pow-
der—and her eyes were rimmed with heavy
black eyeliner. She dressed all in black leather—

9

pants, skirts, vests, jackets. She probably cleaned
her underwear with black shoe polish, assuming
she cleaned it at all.

On my second day I caught her pitching my
books out onto the floor. However, after a frank
exchange of views, during which I momentarily
wished I had a machine gun with me, we worked
out a compromise. I squeezed all my books and
papers in on the tiny top shelf and she used the
rest for her gym shoes, books, and a mysterious
paper bag, which she claimed was her lunch. The
locker smelled odd, of ginger, lavender, grapefruit
peels, and sometimes odors I couldn't begin to
identify, but which I suspected were illegal sub-
stances.

Sharing my locker wasn't all I had to deal
with. Surrounding me were strange faces, strange
voices, and new rules. It was like coming in in
the middle of a movie, and no one telling you
what it was about.

I didn't forget about the group of kids that
made such an impression on me the morning I
arrived, and I felt vaguely pleased when I saw
any of them in the hallway. After only a few days
I could pick out all the members of the clique—
three boys and a girl.

Penn was the tallest and blondest of the four.
Also, there was a boy-girl pair who looked so
much alike I thought at first maybe they were

brother and sister, but then I spotted them kissing one morning in a dark stairwell. Boyfriend and girlfriend, obviously. They both had soft-looking dark eyes and wore clothes so large—big sloppy shirts, baggy pants, socks that sagged around their shoes—that it looked as if they'd been shrunk by some angry witch. Both of them were startlingly good-looking—high cheekbones, straight noses. I found out that the boy was Stephen Garner and the girl was Tessa West.

The fourth, and least attractive, of the group was a red headed boy who was shorter than the others and very pale. He looked as if he spent winter underground. Casey MacNamara was his name. I overheard that he was a super user on Internet, which I figured meant he was a computer whiz.

There was nothing flashy about any of them, unless you counted Penn's car, which was a shiny red Corvette. They didn't seem to care whether anyone noticed them. But for some reason I couldn't stop thinking about them. They seemed to belong to a world more carefree than my own, a world where no one worried or got divorced or went crazy.

Once I had learned to recognize them, I saw them around a lot: Penn at the wheel as his red Corvette skidded recklessly out of the student parking lot, narrowly missing another car, and

Casey MacNamara looking faintly nauseous in the passenger seat next to him. Stephen, Tessa, and Penn cross-legged on the grass searching for four-leaf clovers and plucking the petals off one by one—she loves me, she loves me not. Tessa at the high end of the passageway of Eastman Building calling to Penn and tossing a book down to him.

My second Friday in school, I was walking toward my homeroom as usual when I realized that I was moving against the traffic. "What's going on?" I asked a girl, stopping her as she passed me.

"Senior history assembly," she said.

I had no idea what a senior history assembly was, but I turned around and followed her.

The auditorium was a cavernous place, huge with folding seats on a sloping floor and homeroom teachers standing in the side aisles every five rows or so with clipboards to check attendance. I found my homeroom teacher, got checked off the list, and filed in with the others.

"Somebody told me this was the senior history assembly," I said to a frizzy-haired girl as we filed in. "What's that?"

She looked at me blankly a minute, as if wondering what planet I had flown in from. "Oh, you're new," she said flatly. "It's kind of a tradition." We sat down. "They show slides of all these things we've done since ninth grade. I know it sounds corny, but it's supposed to be hilarious. You know, to see what we used to look like and stuff."

On the stage, standing in front of a filmstrip screen, a guy with a square jaw and impressive muscles tapped on the microphone. An electronic howl ripped through the air. "Testing, testing," he said in a hollow voice. "Well, seniors, this is our last semester at good old Barton High." Catcalls and whoops erupted. "I know we all want to remember the good times we've had," he intoned, "so without further ado, I present to you the senior-class history."

A trumpet sounded. The lights dimmed and a luminous square of white appeared on the screen on stage. Then came a loud click and a fuzzy colored picture appeared. Once the projectionist adjusted the focus, I could see it was a picture of a crowd of kids in front of the school. I heard a guitar playing, and to my surprise I realized that Penn Parrish sat on a stool at the edge of the stage. He was positioned in the unlit part of the stage. A guitar rested on his left knee and a microphone had been placed in front of him. His face was in shadow, but I had no trouble recognizing him. Looking up at him on the lighted stage I felt as if I were peeking in his bedroom window through binoculars. It was a strange one-way intimacy. I felt so close to him, yet he had no idea that I even existed.

The projector behind us clicked and the scene on the screen changed—this time art students were standing in front of easels splashing paint on canvas. In rapid succession were slides of a class sitting on the grass, a football scrimmage, a clutch of girls in pouffed satin evening dresses with dazed-looking guys standing behind them, kids mugging for the camera on the open passageway of Eastman, kids in computer class, kids in the cafeteria. Over the steady background of the guitar music, the auditorium buzzed. Everyone was talking and laughing, reminiscing. It was a game I couldn't play. Since I couldn't pick out people I recognized in the pictures, either, the slide show got boring fast.

Suddenly the girl next to me said disapprovingly, "I think that's in poor taste." I glanced up at the screen, expecting to see kids half-naked or waving beer cans, but the slide looked very innocent, just a couple of girls in T-shirts and shorts clowning for the camera. One of them was holding a hose. There were puddles on the ground and a row of cars in the background.

"That's the sophomore car wash," someone said.

It was not the best picture. Still, I realized

that the girl on the left, her arm flung affectionately around the petite blonde, was Tessa West.
The sun was directly overhead and her eye
sockets were holes of darkness, but she was rec-
ognizable all right—the classic chin and neat
little nose. Suddenly I noticed that the guitar
music had stopped. So had the slide projector.
Kids hooted. The image of the two girls tipped
on its side, then jiggled up and down on the
screen.

"Come on," said the boy on my right. "The
machine's stuck and they haven't even gotten to
the pictures of the cheerleaders yet. Figures."

"They should have pulled that picture of
Laurie Jenkins," the frizzy-haired girl insisted.

The boy leaned over me as if I weren't there.
"I don't see why," he said. "That's another one of
your dumb ideas!"

"I think it's sick! They could be dragging her
body out of the lake this very minute!"

"They've already dragged the lake and
nothing was in it, stupid." The boy sneered.
"Shows how much you know. So Laurie didn't
go drown herself there. Anyway, that car wash
is a part of senior history. You don't go and
change history just because some dumb girl ran
away."

The show was on again. The projector had
been unjammed and a different picture was on

the screen—boys wearing sheets draped as togas. Latin Club, I guessed.

"I don't care what you say. I think it's morbid," muttered the girl to my left.

"What do you bet somebody gets a postcard from Laurie next week?" the boy said. "You've always got to make a big deal out of everything, Jessica. Everything's some big catastrophe."

"Shhh!" several people hissed at them, and the boy sat back in his seat, the argument subsiding. The next slide had been taken at a dance, and I was surprised to see it was a picture of the frizzy-haired girl and the boy on my right embracing under what looked like an arbor of paper flowers. Startled, I glanced first at one of them and then at the other. They sat in stony silence, arms folded over their chests. Their wooden expressions were so close to matching that they could have been bookends.

The slides flipped by steadily now and Penn's guitar played on. At last it was over. The screen went blank, and the square-jawed boy strode back on stage. "And there it is, folks—the story of our lives," he said. "Now let's hear it for our projectionist, Scott Davis!" Boos erupted around me, but our master of ceremonies was unfazed. "And let's give a hand to the music man!"

A spotlight fixed Penn in its glare. Startled,

he looked off to the wings. There was a scattering of applause. He slid off the stool and slipped between the curtains, disappearing at once.

"That was Penn Parrish playing the guitar, wasn't it?" I asked the girl next to me.

"Huh?" She turned her freckled face toward me. "Yeah. Do you know him?"

"Not exactly," I said.

"He drives a Corvette. Couldn't you just die? I wish my folks would give me a Corvette."

Kids were filing out of the auditorium, and I joined the crowd. I wished I could figure out some way to meet Penn.

As far as my classes went, things looked equally bleak. I was taking all the hardest subjects—Physics, A.P. English, A.P. European History. I signed up for them in a reckless desire to put the lame academics of Covenant Day School behind me. I didn't have the background for the courses, and when the school finally got my transcript, they'd see that what I'd been studying before were courses like Making Life Decisions and God's Work in History. I caught on pretty quickly, though, and I'd always read a lot, so I hoped I could squeak by. Inside my mild-mannered exterior the soul of a kamikaze pilot must have been struggling to express itself in some sort of grade-point-average death wish.

Since I didn't know anybody yet, and my dad was always out with some woman, I had lots of time to attempt to keep up. Saturday morning I went to the main library on Branch Street. As I filled out a library card application, I turned around and spotted Casey MacNamara and Penn Parrish in the next room.

Penn was reading at a table beyond an archway, framed by a carousel of paperbacks on one side and the shelves of new books on the other. It was the closest I had ever gotten to him, and suddenly he seemed almost accessible. If I sneezed, he would be bound to notice me. For the first time I regretted not having allergies. Penn was turned three quarters around in the chair, one elbow resting on the table. I could see the newspaper he was reading, the local paper, the *Evening Telegram*.

Its headline read: SEARCH FOR MISSING GIRL CONTINUES.

Three

I know it sounds weird, but standing so close to Penn I felt somehow that I had to get to know him. The headline made me a little chilly, but I forgot it when I looked at that profile and those hands barely touching the newspaper. I felt, even without talking to him, that he was more than just a gorgeous guy. And that if I didn't get to meet him, I'd die. Do people die from longing?

Casey watched as Penn scrutinized the article. Suddenly he jerked the paper out of Penn's hands. "You're getting morbid, do you know that?"

A cold feeling crept up my back. I knew the "missing girl" in the headline must be the girl who had run away, the one whose picture had been in the slide show, Laurie. She was a friend of Tessa West's, judging by the slide. Had she been Penn's girlfriend? I wanted to ask. But I said nothing, and the moment of uneasiness passed. Whatever this girl had been to Penn, that was yesterday, I told myself. It had nothing to do with me now. She wasn't even around anymore.

Casey stood up suddenly. I almost giggled, struck by the idea that he could be an ad for sun block—"Available in Ghostly, a Whiter Shade of Pale, and new Minty Green for computer geeks."

"Are you a resident of the city or the county?" the woman behind the circulation desk asked me.

I had forgotten about her, and I jumped. "The city, I guess."

"We have to be sure because of the allocation of tax money," she said. "Find your street on the map and I'll be able to tell whether it's city or county."

I had only a vague idea of where to find my father's house on the map under the glass top of the circulation desk, and it took me several minutes. It was urgent that I meet Casey and Penn, who were so self-assured in their faded blue jeans and their elegantly cut shirts. But it seemed hopeless. I guess Nikki Warren's discouraging words had struck home. I was interested in them, but I couldn't see any reason why they would be interested in me.

In junior high, I remember, I worried constantly about whom to eat lunch with. By high school I'd given up on being popular. My friends were kids who were in math club and science club. At lunchtime we generally talked about what questions had been on the most recent test. "What did you get on number three?" "No, really? I must have gotten it wrong," was a fair sample of the conversation. But even that thin social success had been ripped out from under me once my parents divorced. At that point my mother started to get weird, acting strangely and saying crazy things.

When I had asked my father to come take me to live with him, even though he had seemed more surprised than pleased at the idea, sheer survival was all I had in mind. I had arrived at my third high school, no longer expecting to have fun. All I wanted was to graduate.

Now unaccustomed feelings stirred in me. I was conscious of the branches of the tree that stretched up near the high windows over the circulation desk. Before long tiny ears of green would bud along its bare gray branches. The world seemed full of promise, and I realized I *did* want to have fun—I needed to. It was my fine new plan.

Everything sang with intense color. The long, polished tables of the library, the gritty floors, the hum of the computer, and the chug of a toilet flushing in a room off the hallway—all seemed like the backdrop for a dazzling adventure, if I could only figure out how to meet Penn and his friends.

"Hi, there. Jenny, isn't it?" croaked a froggy voice.

"Joanna," I corrected, turning to face Nikki Warren.

She smiled at me as if she were determined that I was going to be her good deed for the day. Her cheeks were a healthy pink and a tiny stud earring gleamed on each earlobe. She looked intimidatingly energetic in red jeans and a turtleneck sweater. "How's it going? Have you joined any clubs yet?"

"Sure," I lied. The last thing I wanted to trigger was a sermon about the importance of joining clubs.

"Which ones have you joined so far?" she asked. You would have thought she was doing a survey for the club police.

I went on filling in the blanks on the library application as if I hadn't heard her. Long ago I had discovered there was no need to answer questions I didn't want to. Most people feel too silly repeating themselves to make a big deal out of shaking an answer out of you.

"Extracurricular activities are very important," Nikki went on relentlessly. "It's one of the big things colleges look for."

I began to feel hunted. In my own quiet way I was trying to work out a plan for fitting into this new school, and she wasn't helping. I wished she would go away.

"Don't worry about me," I murmured. "I've got straight A's and I made fifteen hundred on my SATs. I figure all I've got to do now is keep from getting arrested and I'll get into college okay."

She rocked, as if I had revealed that I was Supergirl, Girl of Steel. "Jeez!" she breathed. "That's kind of a ridiculous SAT score."

"I read a lot."

"It's good to be well-rounded, though," she went on, recovering her self-confidence quickly. "Grades and SATs are nothing by themselves. Anybody'll tell you that."

Nobody knew the truth of what she was saying better than me. My grades and SATs were great, and I wasn't exactly wallowing in personal happiness, was I? But I had no intention of spilling my guts to Nikki. I smiled vaguely, bent my head, and concentrated on the application blank. Previous address? I filled in the address in Raleigh where we had lived before my parents split. I wasn't about to put my mother's present address on any form. Name of someone living at different address whom I could give as a reference? I made up a name and then added two digits to my present address to create a plausibly fake address. It didn't matter. I was going to bring the books back on time. What were they so worried about?

I handed the librarian my completed application. She wrote my name and address on the stiff plastic card and stuck a bar code to it. "You can check out three books today. After you bring them back, there's no limit." She handed me the card.

I put it in my wallet and turned around to go get my three books. To my astonishment, Nikki was no longer behind me. Instead Penn Parrish stood there.

He smiled. "Did you really make fifteen hundred on the SATs, or were you just getting rid of Nikki?"

Great. All I needed was to be known as the girl with the high SAT scores. That would be sure death to my new plan for having fun.

Penn reached out and punched Casey's arm. I hadn't noticed that Casey was standing next to him. Penn had that effect on me. "Casey here got a perfect score on the math," he said.

"What can I say?" Casey smirked. "I'm a genius."

"Actually, he's incredibly stupid," Penn confided. "But he's good with numbers. He's an idiot savant. Heard of them? Like in the movie *Rain Man*."

"Get out of here!" howled Casey.

The librarian shot them a hateful look. "Shhh," she hissed. "People are trying to read!"

Penn's and Casey's smiles did not fade. I saw at once that adult authority meant absolutely nothing to them.

Penn held out his library card so I could read his name. PENN PARRISH. ADDRESS—833 ANNERSLEY LANE. EXP. JUNE 1996. I showed him mine.

"Casey here, of course, needs no introduction," Penn said, nodding toward his friend.

"He's jealous." Casey smirked. "It's understandable—I'm an internationally known Yo-Yo champion."

"Shut up, Casey," Penn said good-humoredly. He turned back toward me. "We're on our way to The Bakery. Want to come?"

Casey shot Penn a questioning look.

"Well, why not?" Penn shrugged, meeting his gaze.

Unable to speak, I nodded.

"Leave your car here," Penn said carelessly over one shoulder. "We'll bring you back later."

Four

. . . I would have pinched myself, but he might have noticed. "Want to come?" As if I were one of the gang. Please, I kept thinking, don't let anything spoil this moment. . . .

Penn's Corvette was parked in the handicapped space, close at hand. He flicked the door locks open with a soft click. I scrambled into the passenger seat, sinking low into the padded leather. "Got your seat belt fastened?" Penn asked, revving the engine.

I closed the car door just in time to keep it from being ripped off as Penn pulled out of the parking space. "So, what brings you to our fair city?" he asked.

I made the usual answer about wanting to live with my father for a while. Pounding music

27

poured from four speakers, making me feel slightly numb. I was almost sick with excitement at his invitation and terrified at the speed we were going, so I was in no shape to make intelligent conversation. Not that Penn seemed to be paying any attention. His eyes stared straight ahead, as if he were thinking of something else. We whizzed over the railroad tracks and sped past car washes and real-estate offices, then through residential neighborhoods. Finally we slowed and turned into the parking lot of a plant and seed store.

A large sign saying THE BAKERY stood over the building on the other side of the lot, but judging from the tables on the porch and the menu in the window, I could see that it was really more of a café than an ordinary bakery. "Where's Casey?" Penn asked, getting out of the car and looking around. "Did we lose him?"

Just then a small blue Chevy pulled up next to us.

"Hey, it's Stephen and Tessa," Penn said with a smile. "You can meet them."

Their car was so ordinary next to Penn's Corvette that when Stephen and Tessa got out of it, their socks sagging around their ankles, I had the fleeting impression they were in disguise. They turned their dark eyes on me in mild surprise as Casey's car pulled into the lot.

"Stephen! Tessa!" Casey cried. He leapt out of his own car and bounced over to us. "Where've you guys been?"

"Doing physics homework," said Stephen.

"Dockerty is having a midlife crisis," Tessa said. "He started screaming that we were idiots and then he gave us double the usual homework."

"Yesterday," Stephen explained, "he gave us all compasses and asked us which way was north."

"I was one of the dopes who was pointing in the wrong direction," said Tessa.

"No wonder," said Stephen. "The compasses were pointing all over the place."

"Because of the steel beams in the building, probably," Casey said. "That throws compasses off."

Tessa and Stephen directed poisonous looks at him. "Too bad you weren't there," said Stephen, "to share your insight with us when it would have done us some good."

"How could he expect you to know which way was north if the compasses were all wrong?" Penn asked.

Tessa groaned. "Don't ask me."

"You've got physics second period, don't you?" Casey asked, his eyes narrowing. "I bet the sun was pouring in the window."

"So?" Tessa said with a shrug.

Casey snorted. "Well, then, since you must know that the sun rises in the east, you idiots should have been able to figure out which way was north."

"Casey, I loathe and detest you," said Tessa.

"Yeah, but at least you can't ignore me." Casey grinned.

"Let's get something to eat," Penn suggested.

Tessa's and Stephen's eyes were fixed on me steadily.

"Oh," said Penn. "This is Joanna. She's new in school. I asked her to come along."

There was an uncomfortable silence. I remembered what Nikki had said about theirs being a very tight clique, but this was ridiculous. It seemed as if everybody expected Penn to take a vote before asking me to join them.

"Well, is anybody going to go inside or what?" asked Casey, moving toward the café. "I've never seen such a bunch of slowpokes."

We picked up trays at a stand near the door and filed past the glass cases of The Bakery, where heart-shaped cookies lay on narrow trays between such caloric disasters as slices of German chocolate cake and cream-filled horns of pastry. Penn ordered a dozen assorted cookies. "We'll split them," he explained. He took out his wallet and laid a new ten-dollar bill next to the cash register. I wondered if Penn always picked up the tab—he did drive a Corvette, after all, so he must be rich. We each got herb tea except for Casey, who got cranberry juice as if he had to be different. Then we sat down at a spool-shaped table decorated with flowering chives in a bottle.

"It's not surprising that you beat me over here, the way you drive, Penn." Casey glanced at Penn slyly. "You ought to watch out. You know that?"

A muscle twitched in Penn's cheek. "You've ridden with me enough times, Casey," he said. "You know how I drive." Penn's tension was obvious to me, and to Tessa as well. I felt her tremble next to me.

She sat up abruptly and folded her hands on the table. "Okay, guys!" she said brightly. "We're the four musketeers, remember? All for one and one for all—right?"

I had the oddest sensation that Tessa was warning them of something. But of what? Maybe my presence was making things uncomfortable. Perhaps they felt they couldn't speak freely in front of me. That must be why I had the unsettling feeling that there were hidden meanings in everything they said.

"Of course, you have nothing to worry about, Penn, since your driving record is clean," Casey went on. He turned to me. "Did you know Penn's driving record is perfectly clean?"

"Why does that surprise me?" I murmured.

"Have you been speeding again, Penn? I wish you wouldn't do that." Tessa anxiously looked at Penn. "Slow down and smell the flowers. You'll live longer."

"It's great to have everybody lecturing me," Penn said testily. "I really appreciate it. Why don't we talk about everybody else's faults, okay?"

I wasn't sure why the mention of Penn's speeding had set everyone on edge, but the moment disappeared as quickly as it had arisen. Casey was slowly pouring milk in his tea. "Watch!" he said. "I'm making a convection cell in my cup."

I stared at his steaming cup. I guess "convection cell" was some sort of natural phenomenon involving hot water and cold milk. I wondered if this was a fair sample of his small talk.

"Not more physics, Casey," groaned Tessa. "I don't even want to *think* about physics."

"Tact has never been Casey's strong point," said Penn.

"Man, who cares about tact?" Casey asked, grinning suddenly. "I'm after power, fame, wealth."

"Casey's ambition is to start a computer company," explained Penn. "He wants to be a millionaire."

"Why not? So, what's wrong with wanting money?" Casey asked. "Easy enough to act superior about it if you're already loaded."

"Penn wasn't criticizing you, Casey," said Tessa. "He was only outlining your life's ambition for Joanna, who doesn't know you as well as we do."

Suddenly Casey's eyes bored into me. "So what's your story?" he said. "Isn't this a funny time to transfer into a new school?"

"I was living with my mother," I explained. "And now I'm going to live with my father awhile."

"Never heard of anybody switching high schools in their senior year if they could help it," said Casey. "You are a senior, aren't you? You sure you aren't in the Witness Protection Program?" He laughed suddenly. "You know what the Witness Protection Program is, don't you? It's like, say you're a criminal, and you decide to turn state's evidence—you're going to turn the others in so you can get immunity from prosecution. The government gives you a new identity and a new job in a new community. Your old partners in crime can't get at you nohow."

Stephen made a sudden involuntary movement and his hand knocked over the saltshaker. He swore under his breath. "Shut up, Casey," he said. "Joanna doesn't need an instruction kit for joining the Witness Protection Program."

"You say you just moved here?" Tessa's gaze was friendly. "What do you think of the school so far?"

"I haven't been here very long yet," I said. "I guess I haven't had a chance to form an opinion." Casey's unexpected attack had left me squirming inside, and I was grateful for Tessa's attempt to change the conversation. I had every intention of concealing my crazy mother and the strange, dark house I had left behind. That shouldn't have been a problem. Most kids didn't ask questions about each other's parents. I hadn't expected to meet up with Casey's persistent curiosity. Suddenly I felt thankful that my father was nothing to be ashamed of. In fact, with his hyperactive social life, he wasn't around enough to embarrass me.

"Did you catch what she said?" Casey asked. "'Haven't had a chance to form an opinion.' I love it. So evasive. It makes us all want to know what horrible things she's thinking about us, doesn't it? Tell me, Joanna, is evasion a way of life with you?"

"Lay off, Casey," Penn ordered. He gave

Casey a look that chilled me. It occurred to me that despite a civilized exterior, Penn could be dangerous.

Casey must have thought the same thing, because his voice turned sweeter. "Yes, sir. Excuse me, sir. Just teasing a little bit, all in good fun." He winked at me. "Right, Joanna?"

"I think I'll get another cookie," I said. My lips felt stiff, and it was hard for me to speak. The other kids seemed very nice. I wondered why they put up with Casey. I stood at the counter, nervously pulling napkins out of the dispenser while I tried to gather my courage to go back to the table.

When I got back to the table with my cookie, they all grew silent and looked at me, as if they had been talking about me while I was gone.

"What's with all the napkins?" Casey stared at the stack of paper napkins in my hand. "You know something we don't know? Got advance warning of the great flood?"

"Casey," said Penn quietly. "I said to lay off."

"Jeez!" Casey shook his fingers, as if he were brushing off gnats. "Going to do your knight-in-shining-armor bit, Penn? Spare us. Something tells me Joanna can take care of herself."

"Don't pay any attention to Casey," said Tessa. "He went to charmless school. I always get lots of napkins myself."

I glanced up at her thankfully.

"That looks good," said Penn, peering closely at my cookie. "Can I have your crumbs?"

"Get one for yourself, Penn, old boy," said Casey. "Penn's dad is filthy rich, you know. Cardiac surgeon. Very useful member of society. But not around that much, works wicked hours, especially since Penn's mom took off."

I couldn't stop myself from glancing at Penn when I heard the crack about his mother. I flushed self-consciously when he met my eyes steadily, as if he were rejecting my sympathy. His face had an immobile quality, as if it were a mask. In spite of his throwing up that wall of privacy, I felt an instant sympathy. Neither of us had a real home.

"Have you noticed how families don't eat dinner together anymore?" Casey chattered on. "I mean, personally, I count that as a blessing, but I think it's supposed to be connected with the decay of society and kids getting off on the wrong track—committing crimes, doing drugs, and stuff. Tell us about your family, Joanna." He leaned back in his chair. "Are you an only child?"

"Yes."

"I hope we aren't going to sit around here all afternoon talking about the decay of society," Stephen said, "because after working on physics two hours on a Saturday morning, believe me, Tess and me don't need it. And I've got a history paper to write on top of everything else."

"We were talking about families," Casey said. "I was illustrating a point."

"Just as bad," said Penn. "So, what classes are you taking, Joanna?"

I briefly outlined my class schedule.

"Jeez," said Casey, "it sounds as bad as Stephen's. Hasn't anybody ever heard of the senior slump, or am I the only one that's doing it this year?"

"Nobody's schedule is as bad as mine," said Stephen gloomily.

Penn balanced a spoon on top of the saltshaker. His face had the eerie calm I was to notice at so many of the desperate times ahead, and I found myself leaning toward him expectantly, as if he were about to say something important. But when he spoke, his voice was matter-of-fact. "So, what's going on with you and Nikki Warren?" he asked. "Is she trying to adopt you or what?"

"Resist her," Tessa advised.

"She's not that bad," Penn said.

"She's awful," Tessa argued. "One time she attacked Stephen."

"It was at a party," explained Stephen. "She thought I was making a pass at her—which I wasn't, by the way—and things sort of got out of hand."

Penn glanced at me. "Watch it, you guys. For all you know, Nikki is Joanna's best friend."

"I hardly know her," I put in. "I just got here, remember?"

Casey grinned mischievously. "A blank slate, huh?"

"There's nothing mysterious about me," I said, my mouth dry. Casey was evidently one of those people who got off on making you uncomfortable. When he saw me squirm at the mention of my family, he kept at it. It wasn't the most lovable characteristic.

I was relieved when they lost interest in me and started talking about school again. Penn kept putting in little comments that were supposed to bring me into the conversation. It was pretty hopeless, but I made a game attempt to join in.

"I thought the slide show was really interesting," I said. "I recognized you in one of the pictures, Tessa. You know, the shot at the car wash?"

Silence fell on the table, and I felt momentarily confused. "That was you, wasn't it? With the girl named Laurie? The girl who ran away?"

Tessa licked her lips and looked at Stephen. "That was me, all right." She cleared her throat. "Does anybody have any idea what happened to her?" I asked. I darted an anxious look at Penn. Remembering how frozen he had seemed reading the newspaper account at the library, I wondered if I had made a serious mistake to bring up such a delicate subject.

"The police thought she might have committed suicide," Tessa said. "But we're convinced she ran away." Tessa's frightened eyes now seemed drawn to Penn's face. I couldn't figure out what was going on. If they were so sure she had run away, why was Tessa acting scared?

"None of you have heard from her?" I asked.

"No. Not yet," said Penn. His voice was quiet and his hands lay still on the table as if suddenly the blood had drained out of him.

Casey laughed.

"Laurie had troubles at home," Tessa went on. "We all knew that."

"Her mother's a witch," Stephen said. "She was really mean to Laurie."

"So we weren't exactly surprised that Laurie ran away," said Tessa, her eyes shifting quickly between Stephen and Penn, as if she was looking for cues from them.

"That's not really true," Penn corrected gently. "Of course we were surprised."

"Yes," said Tessa. "But I mean, looking back, I can see there were lots of signs that Laurie wasn't happy."

"Lots," said Stephen.

I glanced at Casey. It had occurred to me that he was being uncharacteristically silent, but I was startled to see that he was smiling.

"It must have been awful having the police looking for her and asking everyone questions," I said.

"Terrible," said Tessa automatically.

"The more we thought about it," Stephen said, "the more we realized that she must have run away."

"Especially since the police didn't find her body," Casey put in dryly. He took out a pair of nail clippers and began running the point of the file under his nails to clean them. I stared at him in repelled fascination. Maybe next he would comb his hair over his food.

"We expect to hear from her any day," Tessa said.

Casey snickered. "In fact, we're practically sure of it."

Five

. . . Was Casey's snicker directed at me? Was everyone mad at me for bringing up Laurie? After all, if she'd been a part of their group forever, who was I to come along and throw her name around? And maybe she really was more to Penn than a friend. Maybe that was why he looked so strange and distant. Then again, they all were acting pretty odd.

Penn reached over and pinched some of my cookie crumbs between two fingers. It was all I could do to keep myself from grabbing his hand and holding tight.

"The trouble with people like Nikki Warren," Penn said, "is that they're believers." My attention snapped sharply back to the conversation at the familiar name. Someone opened a door, and a cold draft raised the hairs on the back of my neck and goose bumps on my legs.

"No, the trouble with Nikki Warren is that she's a goody-goody," said Tessa.

"She's self-righteous. That's what I hate about her," Stephen said.

"But behind that goody-goodiness is just more goody-goodiness," argued Penn. "She really believes in the stuff they taught us in kindergarten. Share. Be nice. Salute the flag. Take turns."

"I loved kindergarten," Stephen admitted. "Those were the days! Before Dockerty and physics. I loved nap time. Playing with blocks was good, too."

Tessa refused to be diverted. "And if you want a contrast to Nikki, there's Koo," she said.

Penn flushed. "Why do you have to drag in Koo? What is this? Bash Penn week?"

Stephen gave me a sly smile. "Penn used to go out with Koo, and Tessa's never going to let him forget it."

"A walk on the wild side!" cried Casey. Strumming an air guitar, he warbled, "Wild thang— you make my heart sang."

"This must be pretty boring for Joanna," Stephen said. "She doesn't even know who Koo is."

"Yes I do," I said. "She shares my locker." I

had seen the unforgettable name Koo Ambler on the basic-math book that lay gathering dust in the bottom of the locker. The news that Koo had gone out with Penn was like a blow. Was this what Nikki had meant when she warned me that I wasn't Penn's type?

"Ouch!" cried Stephen. "You're sharing a locker with Koo? That's bad! Has she stolen anything of yours yet?"

"Well, if you know who she is," said Tessa, "you can see that she's the opposite of Nikki."

"Nikki belted me with her pocketbook," Stephen said.

Penn glanced at his watch. "I'd better get Joanna back to the library."

"We can give her a ride back," Tessa offered.

Penn hesitated, but glanced a bit anxiously at his watch again.

"It's okay," I said.

We went outside together, pushing our hands deep in our pockets and shivering. Wind swept across the graveled parking lot and bent the tall, herblike plants in the flower bed by the steps to the café. Dry leaves rattled as they were blown against the building. Penn got into his car. I caught a glimpse of him pulling out of the lot in a blaze of red as I climbed into Stephen's humble Chevy. Tessa's anxious gaze followed the red Corvette as it drove away.

As we drove, I wanted to ask about Penn and Koo and what had brought them together, but I was afraid that would make my interest in Penn too obvious. Stephen lit his cigarette with the dashboard lighter. His car smelled smoky and was a mess. The backseat was covered with a nubby old blanket and littered with books, pencil stubs, bits of candy, and gum wrappers.

Tessa turned her head. "You can open a window," she told me, "if you want to breathe."

The cold air blowing in from the open window as we drove made the flesh of my face numb. I had only one thought—I wished I were in Penn's car.

"I guess you're pretty surprised that Penn used to go out with Koo," said Tessa.

I jumped guiltily. She had read my thoughts.

"They didn't go together that long," Stephen protested.

"Long enough," retorted Tessa.

"I don't know her," I said cautiously. "But going on first impressions, they do seem very different."

"Opposites attract," said Tessa. "Penn is so, well, self-contained and serious. And Koo is so—"

"Loose," put in Stephen.

"In every sense of the word," Tessa agreed. "Anyway, that's how I see it. It's like Penn needed a way to let go. Especially after his mom took off. He doesn't drink or do drugs or cut classes, so he doesn't have any of the usual outlets. I think that's why he was attracted to her."

I was uncomfortably aware that some people might see me as a self-contained, serious person, too. I wondered if they were trying to give me a gentle hint that I didn't have a hope with Penn.

"Are you trying to tell me something?" I asked.

"Wh-what?" asked Tessa, bewildered.

I shrugged. "I just wondered," I said, "if you were sort of trying to hint that I'm not Penn's type." The breeze from the window stung my eyes, but I managed a watery smile.

"N-no," said Tessa. "Not a bit." I noticed that both she and Stephen had the habit of stuttering when they were rattled. The resemblance between them was uncanny. I rolled up the window and leaned back in the seat. My face was hot with embarrassment and I felt sick from the smoke. Would they tell Penn what I had said? That would be awful. I realized that I should say something. Anything. I cleared my throat. "Somebody said Casey is a computer genius," I said. It was the first harmless subject I could think of.

"That's what they say," said Stephen. An extended silence fell as Stephen turned onto the highway. Considering how chatty they were about Penn's social life, they were strangely silent on the subject of Casey.

Finally Tessa said, "I certainly don't want to give you the idea that Koo is Penn's type. That's not what I meant at all. Most of the girls he's gone out with have been very nice. I, personally, have liked them all. Haven't you, Stephen?"

"All most girls see is Penn's car, though," Stephen went on. "They think when they go out with Penn, it's going to be like starring in a movie. Okay, he's got a Corvette, but it's only a car. Penn isn't all that different from the rest of us."

"The 'Vette was his dad's idea," Tessa said. "A birthday present. Dr. P. wants Penn to develop expensive tastes, so that he'll be forced to be a doctor—that's my theory anyway."

"Penn likes the car," Stephen added.

"Anybody would," said Tessa. "But it's a trap. When you think of it, it's like having a babysitter. A flashy sports car like that is so conspicuous that Penn can't do anything in it that he doesn't want his dad to know about." She shot Stephen a nervous glance. "N-not that he'd want to. But it just goes to show you."

"Beware of cardiologists bearing gifts," said

Stephen. "I guess that's the moral of the story, if there is one. Is there one, Tessa?"

"What happened to Penn's mother?" I asked.

Stephen shrugged. "Midlife crisis."

"It was strange," said Tessa. "She went to her high-school reunion, met up with some guy she'd had a crush on twenty years ago, and decided to run off with him. Penn's dad was like a zombie after it happened. He was so stunned. I mean, who would expect something like that to happen? All the guys at high-school reunions are probably bald and fat."

"Don't mention it to Penn," Stephen warned. "He's very touchy on the subject."

I nodded.

"Well, here we are," said Tessa.

The library was visible through the windshield. In the cool light, the outline of the brick building looked sharp and cruelly bleak. My fingers groped for the door handle and I got out. Wind swept the door closed suddenly and whipped my hair across my face. I pushed the hair out of my eyes. My skin was stinging and the tall pines behind the building made a high whistling sound. I had the half-formed impulse to climb back into Stephen's car.

They waved. "See ya," Stephen called. A gray puff of smoke came from the exhaust of the little Chevy as it left the parking lot.

*   *   *

Am I crazy, or were Tessa and Stephen actually letting their guard down a little? I loved sinking into the backseat, listening to their soft voices. Like they were letting me in on something. And it doesn't seem that Penn went out with Laurie after all. Otherwise, they would have mentioned it, right? I can't really figure out their relationship with Laurie. I mean, they seem pretty cool about her disappearance—no one's really freaked out. I guess I really don't know them that well yet.

They made me pretty uncomfortable at The Bakery. Currents and cross-currents—I couldn't figure out what was going on. But it doesn't seem to matter.

I've never trembled like this over a guy before, or felt so anxious to fit in with a group.

Six

Dear Diary,

It's been a week since that day at The Bakery, and I haven't heard from any of the group. Yesterday I spotted Casey at the end of a hall and waved, but he didn't seem to see me. Other kids walk the halls in groups and pairs and call to each other while I stand alone at a distance and watch.

This afternoon I came home to a silent house, took the mail from the mailbox, and fanned it out on the dining-room table. Every day we get the same collection of bills and junk mail. Then I sat down on the other side of the table and stared at my physics book in dismay. Formulas swam before my eyes. How on earth am I going to pass?

I suppose I expect something to happen.

*A call. A simple hello in the hall. Something.
Instead, they seem to have disappeared from
my life. . . .*

Every day when I got home after school, I
looked around my father's house feeling depressed. It was more like the waiting room at a
doctor's office than a home. Beige carpet covered the floors throughout, and the house was
so new the closets still smelled of fresh shaven
wood. A modern lamp of chrome and ebony
bent over the long leather sofa. The large window in the dining room overlooked a pond and
beyond that was a golf course, an expanse of
close-cropped grass. Sometimes when I glanced
up from my homework, I could see a golfer
trudging up the rise, doll-like in the distance. I
noticed that no matter how cold, windy, or
threatening the weather, there was always a
golfer out there swinging at an invisible ball. I
could make out a flag on the distant green, and
when I opened the kitchen windows, I could
sometimes hear the soft whirring of electric
golf carts.

I told myself that I didn't really like Penn or
his friends. But when I was at school, I found
myself straining to see them. I would feel my
heart skip a beat at the distant sight of close-
cropped blond hair or at a tall boy's stride that

looked familiar, until I drew closer and I felt the sting of disappointment when I realized it wasn't Penn. I caught a glimpse of his car pulling out of the parking lot ahead of me Wednesday afternoon, and as it drove out of my sight, I felt a sharp sense of loss. Going, going, gone.

I was so desperate for someone to talk to that the next day, when I saw Nikki sitting down in the cafeteria, I slapped my tray down across from hers. "Hi," I said. "Are you saving this place?"

"No," she croaked. "My friends should be here soon, but sit down. There's plenty of room. How's life among the rich and famous?"

For a second I was confused. Was she talking to me?

"You two sped right by me in that Corvette," she explained. "I waved but you didn't see me. And Suzy Brenner said she saw you with the whole bunch the other day. Are you hanging out with them much?"

"Not really," I said. "I went to The Bakery with them. That's all."

"Oh?" She was interested. "Are they relieved now that Laurie's written her mom?"

"I didn't realize she had written," I said, sitting down.

"They didn't mention that to you?" Nikki asked, rolling her eyes. "I can't believe it! We had the police swarming all over the place with everybody scared to death she was dead. I'd think they'd be relieved out of their minds to know she's all right. Of course, they're all cold. Not like other people. You couldn't pay me to be friends with any of that bunch."

"I haven't seen any of them since last week," I explained. I wondered, with a sinking heart, if I would ever again have that happy feeling that I was being drawn into their circle. They seemed to have forgotten me.

"Stephen told me you hit him with your pocketbook." I watched Nikki as I opened my milk container. "What happened?"

"He pinched my butt!" she cried indignantly. "I didn't even stop to think. I just turned around real fast and whopped him. My purse had these brass fittings and I guess I must have hit him pretty hard, because his mouth was bleeding. He should learn to keep his hands to himself. Tessa went for me like she was some kind of maniac. She dug her nails into my skin and she practically ripped my hair out. I'm not making this up—it was like something in a horror movie. I think Penn and this other guy finally pulled her off of me. I was sort of in shock." Nikki shook her head. "I don't care what people say. Behaving like that's not normal. I guess it's no wonder Laurie fit right in with that bunch. She was kind of strange, too."

"How was she strange?" I asked. I was faintly irritated that the conversation was turning back to Laurie again.

"Well, to give you an example," Nikki said, lowering her voice, "right before she ran away, I came in the bathroom and there she was sitting there on the floor sobbing her heart out."

"Anybody can have a bad day," I said uncomfortably. I had had a few days myself when I felt like sitting on the floor and sobbing.

"This went beyond having a bad day," insisted Nikki. "She was on the floor of the girls' bathroom! Think about it! Cigarette butts in the corners and wet paper towels sticking to the floor and the wall. I mean, ugh! And then she didn't tell a soul she was leaving, did she? If I were going to run away, I would at least tell my best friend, wouldn't you?"

It had been so long since I had a best friend, I didn't feel qualified to say.

"Of course, I guess it's possible Tessa lied to cover for her," Nikki went on, "but I can't believe that even of Tessa. I mean, the police were dragging the pond behind the school! People were afraid she'd committed suicide. Everybody was worried sick."

"Maybe she and Tessa weren't really all that close," I suggested. "If Tessa spends most of her time with Stephen, maybe Laurie and Tessa just ran around in the same group and that's all there was to it."

"Maybe. Not one of that bunch is really a people person," said Nikki. "That's their problem. They aren't friendly."

I didn't want to hear Nikki's criticisms, so I scarcely paid any attention to her grumblings about the group. A musky smell made me look around suddenly. To my astonishment, Koo pulled out a chair and sat down next to me.

"*Ciao*, lockermate," she said.

For a second Nikki and I both were struck silent. I recovered first, and greeted Koo as cordially as I could manage. The last thing I wanted was for her to set fire to the locker because she was mad at me.

Koo took the top bun off her hamburger, regarded it suspiciously, peeled off the pickle slice, then flipped it over her shoulder. I watched it land on the head of a tall boy at the table behind us. Out of the corner of my eye I saw him pick the ketchup-slick pickle slice out of his hair and suspiciously glare at the friends on either side of him.

Koo fixed her blue eyes on me and delicately scraped one tooth with her fingernail. "I hear Penn picked you up at the library," she said at last, pursing red lips. "I wonder what he sees in you."

To my surprise I was beginning to enjoy myself. It obviously annoyed Koo that Penn had taken an interest in me.

"Give me a break!" Nikki cried. "They're just friends. Koo, didn't anybody ever tell you not to play with your food? Look at what you're doing! That's disgusting."

Koo was stirring peas into her mashed potatoes. As an afterthought, she poured a stream of chocolate milk onto it.

"You act like a third-grader," complained Nikki.

"It's a free country," said Koo.

A hulking boy loomed over Koo and placed his arm in a hammerlock around her neck. "Guess who?"

Koo squeezed her eyes closed. "Tony? Rocky? Jeff?"

The boy swore.

"Wait a minute," Koo said. "I know that voice. Just give me a minute. Tom? Mark?"

"You trying to make me mad, Koo?" He removed his arm and gave her a shove. "Or what?"

She beamed at him. "Gotta go, girls. My man wants me."

"Can you believe that?" Nikki asked as soon as they had left. "One boy after another. I can't even keep track of them. She's awful. I mean, she's beyond awful—she's in a class by herself. I hate to think the impression you're getting of Barton High." She shuddered. "Back when my mom was in high school, nobody even thought of behaving that way."

"I guess that's why they call it the good old days." I glanced over my shoulder. "Personally I think we're lucky that a food fight didn't break out."

"You know, there used to be such a thing as school spirit here," said Nikki wistfully. "Kids wore the school colors and they even had a pep club. Have you ever heard of a song called 'Be True to Your School'?"

I snickered.

"That attitude," snapped Nikki, "is part of the problem. You have to ask yourself, 'What am I contributing?' If you're not part of the solution, you're part of the problem. It's getting to where nobody cares about anybody else anymore. Everybody's out for themselves."

I halfheartedly agreed with her. "But Koo was probably born that way," I added.

A giggling bunch of girls descended on our table. "What was Koo doing?" one of them asked. "We got out of the line and I stood there, like, frozen. I was shaking in my shoes, wasn't I, Tiff? I was scared to death to come over here. Utterly petrified. 'What if she throws her mashed potatoes?' I said to Tiff.

Eeek! I just washed my hair and everything!"

Nikki introduced me. The giggling girls sat down, inquired politely how I liked the school, and then ignored me. The conversation flowed around me while I ate my lunch. They appeared to be intensely interested in various methods of keeping their legs smooth.

"Well, sure wax hurts," a neat-faced brunette said earnestly, "but only for a second when they're ripping it off. Of course, you've got to get somebody who really knows what she's doing. Like, they use this special lotion afterward at the place I go to, it's called Baby Soft, and after that the hair grows in soft."

"Gross," said the girl next to her. "I don't care about soft little hairs. That's totally disgusting. I want *no* hair. I want smooth."

I glanced at her in mild amusement. Mistaking my glance for interest, she politely inquired, "What do you use, Joanna?"

I shrugged.

After that, they ignored me.

When we got up from the table, I actually found myself taking Nikki aside to speak privately with her. "Look," I said, "I understand that you don't like Penn and his friends, but the fact is I need kids to hang out with. It's not like I can run around with Koo."

Nikki choked. "I guess not!"

"So where do I fit in?" I asked. "At the rate I'm going, I could spend the next four months talking to myself."

"You're always welcome to sit with me and my friends," Nikki said with a fake smile. "Actually, you're more an intellectual type. I noticed that right away. I bet you'd fit in with that bunch that belongs to the math club and the science club. How's it going with those clubs you've joined?"

"Great," I lied.

After that, I escaped. I could not believe that I had actually sunk to asking Nikki for advice. That was when I realized I must be closer to cracking up than I thought.

I think that was the day I was at my lowest, most desperate point. After physics class I struck up a conversation with a Middle Eastern exchange student.

"I like America very much," he said. "I like everything except fast food. Young people have much more freedom than in my country. You are very pretty. May I have your phone number?"

Then, after school, I went to the office and humbly asked how I went about joining the math club and the science club. I even jotted down their regular meeting times.

I made my way to the parking lot and got in my car. The sky was black—storm clouds lay over the landscape. Only a thin rim of pale sky showed along the horizon. A half-crumpled sheet of paper whirled in on the gravel and then skidded across the parking lot. This is my life, I thought bleakly. And I'm going to fail physics on top of it. The only bright spot I could think of was that I hadn't given the Arab guy my phone number.

"I thought this car was yours," said a familiar voice.

The blood drained from my head when I saw Penn standing by my car. Quickly I rolled my window down.

"Hi," I said, gazing up at him.

He smiled. "I was kind of hoping I'd run into you one of these days."

"I haven't seen you around school," I said. "Have you been out of town?"

His face went blank for a second.

He smiled at me and shook his head. "I guess this school is too big. You can't be sure of running into somebody even when you're trying to."

"Were you trying to?" My hand reached up to his and my fingers brushed lightly against his.

"Sure." He grinned. "We're going to have to go to The Bakery again one of these days."

I recoiled at the kindly brush-off. "One of these days" meant "You're a nice person but I'm in no rush to spend any time with you."

"That would be fun," I said brightly. I turned the keys in the ignition. I might be desperate, but I refused to be pathetic. My car's motor roared.

"Are you in a hurry or something?" Penn asked, stepping back from the car.

I nodded. "Catch you later." I caught a glimpse of my bright smile in the rearview mirror.

As I pulled out of the parking lot, I felt so awful I could have sat on the floor of the girls' room and wept wildly amid the sticky paper towels.

Seven

. . . I might actually be able to get a grip if Penn didn't keep disappearing and popping up and disappearing again. Maybe if he stayed disappeared, he'd actually be doing me a favor. Then maybe my head would stop spinning from hope and letdown and letdown and hope. . . .

When I got home, the phone was ringing. The only phone calls I usually got were from my father's secretary, saying he was going to be working late, so I didn't break my neck getting to it.

"Hello?" I said into the receiver. I tossed my physics book on the kitchen table.

"Joanna? It's Penn. Did I do something to make you mad? You rushed off all of a sudden."

61

My heart exploded under my ribs. "No. I was just in a hurry, that's all."

"Are you still in a hurry? Or can you talk?"

"I guess I can talk." I hooked a kitchen chair closer with one foot and collapsed onto it.

"Do you think you could go out to dinner with me tonight?" he asked.

"Okay," I said. The clock fell off the wall with a loud clatter. I stared at it in amazement. Until that instant I had never believed in telekinesis.

"What was that?" asked Penn.

My heart, I thought. "Nothing," I said. "The clock fell."

"I know how it feels." I could hear a smile in his voice.

"It's short notice," he began.

I interrupted him. "That's all right. My father works late, a lot. In fact," I said suddenly, "he hardly seems to have noticed that I've moved in. I'd love to have dinner with you."

"That's great. Do you like Chinese?"

I made inarticulate noises of agreement, and Penn said he'd pick me up at six. As soon as I'd hung up, I ran to my closet and tore through it frantically. I wondered what sort of clothes Penn would find attractive. Since my only guidelines were Koo's black leather on the one hand and the baggy shirts Tessa favored on the other, I had no clue. Jeans always work, I reminded myself.

After I showered and dried my hair, I decided on a loose-woven, Indian-looking shirt with gold threads hidden among the scarlet and blue. Then, with intense concentration, as if it were a major life decision, I selected my earrings. I was big on earrings. I settled on some I had bought at a Grateful Dead concert—a dangling silver pair with tiny bells.

Ready way too early, I sat nervously on the leather couch, listening for the sound of Penn's car. Out the big window in the back of the dining room I could see the dark clouds hanging low, the sky a dramatic play of shadows and light. A small fluttering flag at the thirteenth hole of the golf course stood sharply defined in the strange light. The weather was about to break into a storm.

I jumped at the click of the lock as my father walked in. I looked at him in blank surprise.

"Any interesting mail?" he asked. He had grown a small mustache since the divorce.

"No. No, I thought you'd be working late."

"Not tonight." He leafed through the circulars on the table. He wore an expensive digital watch that could tell whether it was high or low tide in Borneo and also at exactly which nanosecond the moon would be full. He had explained every dial to me once, mostly, I think, because he couldn't come up with anything else to say to me. "I certainly wish I hadn't contributed to the fight against muscular dystrophy," he said. "Looks like I'm on the mailing list of every disease in the country." He sorted the mail one by one into a wastebasket. "Cystic fibrosis. Spina bifida. It's depressing. What do you say? Shall we send out for pizza or stick something frozen in the microwave?"

"I've sort of got plans for the evening," I blurted.

He was visibly relieved. "Oh. Well, maybe I'll ask Jennifer to come over." His gaze followed the small figure of a distant golfer. "What time'll you be getting in?" he asked casually.

"I'm not sure. This guy and I are going to dinner. I don't exactly know when I'll be in."

"I may go out," he said, "so be sure and take your house key. So how is school? Okay?"

"I'm going to fail physics."

"If you want to get a tutor, go ahead. If they still do that kind of thing." He smiled vaguely at me. "Well, it's up to you. I don't want to push." He tore open an envelope. "Do we need a new carpet cleaner? They're offering a once-in-a-lifetime deal."

I looked down at the carpet, its new-carpet fuzz still collected in beige clouds all over the living room. "No," I said. "I don't think so."

"I guess I'll go call Jennifer," he said.

He was on the phone in his room when the doorbell rang. I threw open the door.

"Hello," Penn said.

"Hi." I had intended to seem cool, but I could feel my mouth stretching into a broad smile.

Penn cast a curious glance through the half-open door. "Your father doesn't come out and check on the guys you go out with?"

"Evidently not," I said, closing the door behind me. "My father's too busy with his own social life."

"People ought to finish with all that before they get married," Penn said.

"I agree, but he hasn't asked for my opinion. I just keep saying to myself over and over that it's very sad to see a middle-aged person on the prowl."

"Yes," said Penn sadly, and I suddenly remembered about his mother and wondered if I had said the wrong thing.

As we walked down the front steps, wind rattled the leaves overhead. I could taste rain in the air.

Behind Dad's car was Penn's Corvette, its red finish mulberry dark in the gathering dusk. Penn opened the car door for me.

My head jerked back as we zoomed down the street with a rocket start. I happened to glimpse the odometer. "Boy, you've put some miles on this thing, haven't you?" I had noticed the odometer reading when he drove me to The Bakery the week before. It had certainly taken a big leap since then.

He glanced at me in surprise. "Do you usually go around reading people's odometers?"

"I know it sounds weird," I said. "I can't help noticing numbers. I remember them. Where'd you go that put seven hundred miles on your odometer?"

"Nowhere in particular," he said. "I like to drive. That's all. I think better when I'm driving. Don't you?"

"No," I confessed. "Mostly I think about morbid things like if the oncoming truck crosses the center line, I'll soon be smashed against a thousand pounds of molten steel."

"Are you serious?" He glanced at me.

"Completely. I have a high anxiety level."

He took the hint and slowed down. "Looks like this isn't a match made in heaven, doesn't it?"

"Don't give up yet!" I said in alarm.

He grinned, and I blushed hotly.

"You know when we went to The Bakery that time," he said, "I couldn't stop looking at you and I kept wishing the others would shut up so I could concentrate better on that funny little curl that messes up your hair at the temple."

I fingered my cowlick self-consciously. All the

rest of my hair is pretty straight. I'm constantly working at that one little place with the blow dryer, trying to make it behave, but it won't stay straight no matter what I do. What makes me feel particularly weird about it is that my mother has a curl in that exact same place.

"I was sure you were sitting there deciding that you couldn't stand my friends," said Penn.

"Oh, no," I said faintly.

"Casey can be a little rude sometimes. He doesn't realize he's hurting people's feelings. He's just curious. He's always taking things apart, but he doesn't realize you can't take people apart the way you can computers."

I thought Casey was deliberately nasty, but I couldn't admit that to Penn, so I murmured something that would pass for agreement.

Penn shot me a look. "Sometimes when a person is quiet, you end up imagining all kinds of stuff about them. You know, like you persuade yourself that they're crazy about you and all they're interested in is your car. Follow me? I wish you would come right out with what you really think."

"Casey's not a nice person," I said.

"No," he said after a while. "Maybe not. I see what you mean. But nice people are kind of dull, aren't they?"

We pulled up in front of a sign that spelled

out HUNAN GARDEN in pink neon. Inside were
Formica tables in booths and by the cash register
were cheap lacquer fans, cellophane bags of fortune cookies, and dolls dressed in shiny satin.

We sat down on plastic banquette seats in a
booth. "I always get the stir-fried chicken and
vegetables or the moo goo gai pan," he said. "You
can't live with a cardiologist and still eat pork."

I got sweet-and-sour pork. I hoped to give the
impression that I was used to living dangerously.

I wondered why Penn would ever think girls
were only interested in his car. I would have
been interested even if he rode a skateboard.
The only other time I had met a guy that was
even half as attractive was in the ninth grade,
and it turned out he wasn't after me but a friend
of mine.

The food came, but I scarcely noticed it. I
was happy being with Penn. I liked to look at
him, but it wasn't just that. We had a lot of
things to talk about, too. He was one of the few
guys I'd met who read books that weren't as-
signed in school. He knew all sorts of fascinating
things, like that in space a ray of light goes
around a black hole in a curve because the black
hole has so much gravity that it bends the light.
The light goes around and around, so that if you
could stand at the edge of a black hole holding a
flashlight, you could see the flashlight ahead of

you and behind you, too. That sort of idea has always interested me.

"You will meet a handsome stranger," I read from my fortune cookie.

Penn frowned. "You'd better not," he said.

"I should have gotten that fortune a couple weeks ago," I said impulsively.

Penn smiled and showed me his. "You are skilled at dealing with people," it read.

"This fortune cookie must belong to somebody else," he said. "I never know what to say to people. Now, Casey just says any old thing. I could stand to be a little more like him."

"Don't change," I said, my eyes meeting his. I wanted to lean over that wobbly Formica table and kiss him. When I looked into his eyes I felt myself longing for the touch of his hand. "Do you believe in fate?" I asked suddenly.

Penn hesitated. "I'm not sure." His eyes gazed into mine as if he were looking for the answer.

After dinner we headed outside into the pitch-black night. Rain poured beyond the awning of the restaurant. The sign that said HUNAN GARDEN glowed pinkly over our heads, and a fan of light from the glass front door made weird spidery shadows on our legs. Penn's gray eyes were dark in the shadows.

He bent to kiss me, and having him close felt right to me as nothing had ever felt right in my life. His hand was warm when he brushed the hair out of my face and kissed me again.

"I wanted to do that in there over the table," he said thickly, "but I thought, Wait a minute, you'll fall in the moo goo gai pan."

I laughed unsteadily. My heart was pounding so hard, I was afraid he would hear it. "It's pouring," I said. "We're going to get soaked."

"You stay here and I'll drive the car up." He pulled his jacket over his head and ran for the car. The jacket was tinged with pink under the neon. It blurred, and Penn disappeared into the dark rain.

It seems funny, but even while I was standing there on the wet sidewalk, still not over the tingling feeling I got from kissing Penn, I was thinking of how Nikki had said I didn't have a chance with him. Tessa had hinted at the same thing, too. I was gloating. No doubt about it—they were going to be surprised.

A minute later, the low red car glided up to the curb and I got in, stepping over the rushing water beside the curb. I felt a guilty thrill of pleasure. Stephen was right—it was as if I were stepping into a movie.

The radio was turned on, but it was between channels and the sound was indistinct and studded with static. Water hissed under our wheels and the windshield wipers moved steadily with a monotonous swish-clack.

"I'm going to drive slow on account of the rain," Penn promised.

"Good." I smiled at him. Rain streamed down the windshield, drowning the form and shape of everything outside.

"I feel like we're in a different world," Penn said, glancing at the streaming windshield. "We could be on the open sea, floating in the rain."

I knew at once, in a quick rush of sympathy, what he was feeling. I had felt it in the restaurant. We were so intent on each other that the clinking of plates and silverware, the waiters' whispered voices, and the murmurs from nearby booths had faded out and ceased to exist. "I know what you mean," I said softly. "It's this drifting feeling. The feeling that nothing else matters but this instant. I noticed it, too."

"It's like there's no one else around." He smiled at me. "Just you and me."

The cold blue light of a police car blinked suddenly ahead of us like a chill warning. Penn slowed the Corvette almost to a crawl, and we passed the blue flashing light and another car that was pulled over on the side of the road.

Penn's face had darkened. "Did you read how they caught those bank robbers in Raleigh?" he asked abruptly.

I shook my head.

"It was late at night and these guys were going under the speed limit. Don't you love it?" He did not sound amused, but he glanced quickly at me to see if I had caught the irony. "A patrol car stopped them because they thought it was suspicious behavior. Nobody obeys the speed limit after midnight, but bank robbers are so stupid. That's why they always get caught."

"Don't walk me up to the door," I said when the Corvette stopped in front of the house. "You'll only get soaked."

"I'm already soaked."

"Well, you'll get more soaked."

Dad's car was gone. He and that Jennifer person were over at her place, I supposed.

I had hoped Penn would kiss me again, but he made no move to.

"Good night!" I said when he didn't speak.

He looked startled at the sound of my voice and smiled at me suddenly with a warmth that took my breath away. "Good night," he said. "Thanks for coming."

I ran up the front steps, rain pouring on my face, and stepped into the still darkness of my father's house. I stood inside the closed door a moment catching my breath and feeling shaky. Something good was almost mine, if only I could hold on to it, I thought. Like a hand and glove, Penn and I belonged together. In that moment standing at the front door, I realized that nothing mattered to me except the attraction I felt toward Penn. It was scary, because suddenly I knew that I could never be happy with anyone else. And beneath that happiness, I already sensed the terrible times that lay ahead.

Eight

Dear Diary,

You'd think I'd be able to concentrate and tell you about kissing Penn, but I keep losing that train of thought. Police, jails, crime, and punishment—what's going on? These totally unromantic subjects keep cropping up in my conversations with Penn. I wonder why? Does he feel guilty about speeding? Or about going with Koo? About being attracted to me? What an infinite number of things there are to feel guilty about!

And it's not only Penn. When Casey made that strange crack about the Witness Protection Program, Stephen got so rattled, he knocked over the salt. I wonder if the four of them lied to the police to protect

Laurie after all, as Nikki suggested. For a group that seems so into clean living that they won't even touch coffee, they sure are jumpy. You'd think they were guilty of something.

Even though I looked all over for him, I didn't see Penn at school on Friday. I wished we had a class together, so I could have been sure of running into him. Tessa and Stephen were making out by their favorite stairwell after homeroom and didn't notice when I smiled in their direction. I decided against interrupting them to ask if they'd seen Penn around.

It would have been fun to grab hold of Nikki and announce that Penn was mine, all mine, but now, in the cold light of day, I felt suddenly insecure. What if Penn disappeared from my life completely? The ground under me felt unsteady. Maybe this small happiness was going to vanish as quickly as it had appeared.

The rain had brought one of those warm days that sometimes appear, even in winter, in the South. When I got home, I saw that our neighbor across the street was taking advantage of the nice weather to wash his car. He was a huge guy, overweight but with muscles, like an out-of-shape football player. He was wearing jeans and a dirty sleeveless T-shirt, which was soaking wet. I noticed his hair was tied back in a ponytail. An Irish setter leapt about him, scattering water droplets. He looked so intimidating. I hesitated a bit about going out to the street to get the mail. This is silly, I told myself as I headed outside. It's ridiculous to be frightened to go into my own front yard.

"Hey!" he called.

I was so startled, I let the wooden mailbox swing closed with a sharp crack.

"Hey, come here!" he yelled.

"Me?"

"Yeah, you! Who else is around?"

Reluctantly I walked across the street. Once I was closer, I realized that the boy was about my age. He had the beginnings of a stubble of mustache on his upper lip, but his cheeks were downy and marred by a couple of zits. He wiped a forearm across his brow, then took a blue rag out of his hip pocket and wiped his face.

"You're the new girl in my homeroom, right?"

"Am I?"

"Sure. I'm Bobby Jenkins. I know your name," he said. "I hear it every day when they call roll."

I could hardly believe I had overlooked somebody so huge.

"Down, Blue!" he ordered the Irish setter.

Bobby's gaze traveled over me. "My mom is out of town and I'm having a party tonight. Why don't you come on over? It's going to be a mob scene. Last time half the school showed up."

"I appreciate the invitation," I began.

He laughed. "Heck, it's not the kind of party you invite people to. The word just goes out and they come. It's going to be a huge bash. Great way to meet people."

"I'll see," I said. "I've got a lot of work to do."

"Nobody works on Friday night. Get serious." He regarded me with obvious curiosity. "Looks to me like you'd be dying to get out. Aren't you alone over at your house practically all the time?"

"I'm not afraid of being alone," I said. "I have a gun and I'm a crack shot." I was ready to invent a Doberman pinscher, too. I didn't like his interest in how much I was alone.

The setter thrust its long nose at my crotch. "Nice doggie," I said, pushing him away. "He's a gorgeous color. Nice doggie!"

"He's not really mine," said Bobby, his brows drawing together darkly. "He belongs to my stepsister. I'm watching him while she's away."

I suppose it was something in his tone that caused me to make the connection. Jenkins. Laurie Jenkins had been Tessa's friend, the one who ran away from home. Could Laurie and Bobby's stepsister be one and the same person? The setter was lapping soapy water from the bucket. It shook its head, spattering us with droplets.

"Get out of that, Blue," Bobby cried, snatching up the bucket.

"Have I met your stepsister?" I asked, feeling slightly anxious. "What's her name?"

"Laurie," he said abruptly. He dumped the sudsy bucket onto the driveway and took a few quick strides over to the spigot to turn off the water. "Come on, Blue."

He stomped up the stairs, trailing water. The setter followed him.

When I got back to the house, I began a new diary entry:

> *I just met Bobby Jenkins, the boy across the street. He muttered something about wanting to let the car dry before he waxed it, but I had the feeling that he wouldn't have been in such a hurry to get inside if I hadn't asked about Laurie. It certainly is peculiar that her name has such a drastic effect. All anyone has to do is say "Laurie Jenkins" and everybody goes to pieces. Strong boys disappear, kids in assembly get in arguments, Penn's face goes blank, Stephen and Tessa knock things over. What can she be like? I wonder if she was as interesting when she was around as she is now that she's gone.*

Am I jealous? Maybe. I get sick of hearing her name, and yet in spite of myself I sometimes feel I want to know all about her. In that slide of the car wash she looks completely ordinary. I wouldn't have guessed that her running away would leave such a hole in so many lives. Sometimes when her name comes up, it's as if a cold breath is blowing on the back of my neck and I have the eerie feeling that something is wrong. Why don't people want to talk about her? What's going on?

I was still writing in my diary when my father got in from work. I realized immediately that he looked different somehow, but it took me a second to figure out what it was. His fair hair had receded a lot in the past number of years, giving him a very high forehead. Now evenly spaced sprigs of hair, each with a dark angry-looking root, were filling that space.

Noticing that my gaze was fixed on his hairline, he flushed. "Hair transplant," he said briefly. "It's a very simple procedure. I got it done on my lunch hour." He patted his stomach unconsciously. "I'm thinking of buying a NordicTrack. They tell me that's a good way to stay in shape. Some of the guys at work swear by it. I'm not going to have time to eat tonight. I'm just going to throw a few things in a suitcase and then I've got to get off to the airport."

I followed him back to his room. He moved swiftly around the room, tossing calculators and notebooks into his suitcase.

"Where are you going?" I asked.

He opened a bureau drawer and lifted out a stack of neatly folded underwear. "Didn't my secretary call you?" he asked.

"I've been at school all day," I pointed out. "How could she call me?" I generally spent more time talking to my father's secretary than to my father.

"I guess that slipped my mind. Well, Hankerson came down with the flu and I'm filling in for him at a meeting in Charlotte." He touched his new hair self-consciously with his palm. "Couldn't come at a better time, actually. This is going to look more natural in a few days." He took a suit and two shirts from his closet and zipped them into a garment bag.

He was out of the house in five minutes. My father was nothing if not efficient. I stood at the front door and watched him pitch his bags into the backseat of his car. "Have a safe trip," I said.

He smiled up at me, a youthful, unfocused smile. He reminded me of someone, but for a minute I couldn't think who. It was his slightly vacant, cheerful look that was so familiar. Then it came to me. My father reminded me of a television weatherman.

I went back into the house and stared at the telephone, willing it to ring. But it refused. Penn did not call. I was afraid he had decided he didn't like me. It was a painful thought, and I tried not to dwell on it. Our refrigerator had a full stock of fancy frozen dinners—chicken divan, turkey tetrazzini, mushroom linguine—that all tasted the same: salty, creamy, and mushy. I microwaved one and read the newspaper while I ate, hoping to keep my mind off the bland food. My father's hair transplant and sudden concern about getting into shape gave me a funny feeling. Could it be that he was interested in a much younger woman other than Jennifer? With my luck, I thought gloomily, the new love of his life will turn out to be Koo.

It hadn't been dark long when I noticed the cars converging on our neighborhood. Three strange cars were in our driveway, which would have alarmed me if I hadn't seen that cars were parked all up and down the street. Some were even pulled up onto lawns. Music blasted from the house across the street. Bobby's party was in full roar.

I sat in the living room for a while, working

on my homework and trying to ignore the ever-increasing din outside. In an effort to catch up in physics, I was beginning at the front of the textbook and trying to work my way gradually to where the class was now. But the textbook wasn't exciting enough to distract me from the steady drumbeats coming from across the street. I parted the slats of the blinds with two fingers and peered outside. Light spilled out of the tall front windows of Bobby's living room, shedding an eerie glow on his front yard. Figures milled around the cars and streamed up the front steps. I was surprised at how envious I felt. Bobby wasn't spending Friday night alone with his physics book, at any rate.

I'd never been to a wild party with no parents around before. It might be fun. I had been invited, after all. I owed it to myself to take a look. Afraid I would lose my nerve if I thought about it too much, I tucked my keys into my jeans pocket, shrugged on my jacket, and headed out the front door.

The music grew louder when I stepped outside, and the cool night air stung my cheeks. The neighborhood looked like a giant parking lot. I threaded my way between cars and went up Bobby's driveway. Wrinkling my nose, I pushed the front door open. Furniture had been pushed up against the wall to clear a space in the middle of the dining room, and several couples were dancing. One or two of the kids I saw looked vaguely familiar. Bobby's huge form appeared in front of me.

"Hey!" he whooped, throwing a bear-sized arm around me. "Help yourself to the keg in back," he yelled in my ear. "Glad you could make it." To my relief, he quickly moved on to embrace another girl who was just coming in.

The layout of Bobby's house was not that different from ours, so I was able to find the kitchen easily. It was quieter in there, and I figured if I looked I might be able to find a diet cola. Sure enough, the bottom shelf of the refrigerator was full of canned soft drinks. I wondered what I was going to do with myself while I waited a decent length of time before leaving. It did not look like the sort of party where people had actual conversations. I flipped open the can and ventured out into the living room. A couple were writhing on the leather chair, their hands buried in each other's hair as if they were demonstrating the art of scalp massage, but I managed to inch past them to the bookcase. I knelt beside it, peering at the spines of the books in the dim light. *How to Make Your Sales Sizzle in Fifty Days. Getting to Yes: The Art of Negotiation. Surviving Divorce.* Bobby's mother was obviously into self-help books. One slender paperback looked different, and I pulled it off the shelf. *A Pale View of Hills.* The front was decorated with an outline of a cherry tree branch and a couple of shadowy figures. Somehow it didn't look like the sort of thing that would interest either Bobby or the owner of all those optimistic self-help books. I flipped it open. Written inside the cover in round letters was "To Bobby, with all my heart and soul forever. Laurie." Not a very sisterly-sounding inscription, I decided.

Nine

. . . I went to a bookcase, pulled out the one book that didn't fit, and it had Laurie's name in it! I am not superstitious, but that gave me chills. It was as if I had been led to the bookcase so that I would read the message Laurie had written. It gave me a strange feeling. I've never met the girl, but I can't seem to get away from her. I quickly slid the book back in its slot on the shelf as if it were burning my fingers.

A tap on my shoulder startled me and I swung around. A skinny boy was perched on the arm of a couch, oblivious to the affectionate couple sprawled behind him. "I've been hoping you would show up," he said blearily. "Ever since I saw you that first day in history, I haven't been able to stop thinking about you—your eyes, your skin—" His voice was unsteady, but his hands were reaching straight for me.

I stood up quickly to avoid his clumsy groping.

"What did you say your name was?" he asked, looking up at me with unfocused eyes.

Unfortunately I was penned in. On one side I was blocked by a standing lamp, on the other by the couch with the couple on it. The skinny guy was directly in front of me. I was about to move the lamp to make my getaway when suddenly a girl appeared and claimed him.

In the heat of the living room, my diet drink had grown warm. I made my way back to the kitchen. Koo was at the sink, touching up the paint on her talons. The fluorescent kitchen light made her mouth and nails magenta. She did not look up from her task as ice cubes clattered loudly into my glass. "Do you know Bobby very well?" I asked her.

She turned and regarded me with cold suspicion. "I guess. Why?"

"Isn't Bobby's stepsister the one who ran away from home?"

"Yeah," said Koo, her eyes narrowing. "Why do you want to know?"

"Just nosy," I said amiably.

I probably would have tried to find out more,

but when a dark-eyed girl with a gold stud on one nostril came into the kitchen, Koo screwed the cover onto her nail polish, popped it into a leather pouch, and sauntered out.

"Do you know if they've got any diet drinks?" the dark girl inquired in a nasal voice.

"On the bottom shelf of the fridge."

She opened the refrigerator and began rummaging through the collection of cans. "My people don't drink alcohol," she informed me. Popping open a can as she stood up, she added, "Isn't this party the grossest? In my opinion, if these guys could keep in touch with the big basic rhythms, they wouldn't have this pathetic compulsion to get wasted every weekend. Like me—I always celebrate the summer solstice. Winter solstice, too, unless it's too cold to go outside naked." She took a gulp of her drink.

I vaguely wondered who "her people" were.

"Of course, society tries to get us to give up our ethnic identity," she went on darkly. "Society exploits and corrupts everything it touches. Nothing is pure, nothing is close to the earth, anymore, and another thing—" Suddenly she stopped midstream. "Wait a minute. I know where I've seen you before. You were at The Bakery with that computer geek and those guys he hangs out with. They are *weird*."

The girl with the nose stud who runs outside naked during the summer solstice is telling me Penn and his friends are weird? "I think they're kind of nice," I said.

"You'd better watch out." She took a swig from her diet cola. "I hear they do drugs."

I thought about their herb tea and laughed.

The girl's face clouded. "Are you laughing at me?"

"They don't do drugs," I said. "You're wrong." I turned to leave; I'd had enough.

To my astonishment, when I was coming out of the kitchen, I bumped into Penn. He dusted brown drops of my diet soda off his shirt and smiled. "I kept calling your house, but all I got was a busy signal. I came on by, but you weren't home. For a second there, I was pretty lost. I had been so sure you'd be home—since the phone was busy."

"That's odd," I said. "Maybe you dialed the wrong number." I knew I was smiling foolishly, but I couldn't help it.

"Well, anyway, I could see there was a big bash going on over here, and I was hoping I'd find you." He looked around at the tangle of people. Music was blaring, but I had no trouble hearing what he said. Penn focused my attention amazingly.

"Hey," cried Bobby. He blocked Penn's way,

his arms folded over his chest. "Who invited you?"

"I was just leaving," said Penn. He put his hand on my shoulder and piloted me past Bobby.

The hot bodies of the guests were packed close together, and as we squeezed our way through the crowded living room, the smell of sour sweat and beer made me gag. "Excuse us, excuse us," I muttered as we stumbled through the crowd. At the door we had to step over another couple who were glued together.

The fresh air outside was like a drink of cold water. Behind us the closed door vibrated with the resounding beat of the music. The night was velvety black and soft after the heat and deafening noise of the party.

"Bobby doesn't seem to like you much," I commented.

"That makes us even, then. I don't like him much either."

Penn drove us to a donut shop, where we ordered lemon-filled donuts and hot chocolate. A man and a woman sat in the booth at the back. We took our tray to the front booth. I watched neat coils of steam curl up from the cocoa as I bit into my donut. "I didn't know Bobby was related to your friend Laurie Jenkins," I said.

"Who's been telling you about Laurie?" Penn asked sharply.

"Nikki told me about it. She said Laurie's mother finally got a letter from her."

"That's what I hear."

"Why did she run away?"

Penn made a helpless shrug. "I don't know. Why does anybody run away? Things were rough at home, I guess."

"I thought you guys were friends. Didn't you know her pretty well?"

"I don't know." He hesitated. "I'm not really sure what it means when you say you know somebody. You can know who their third-grade teacher was, know their birthday and how they like their pizza, maybe you can even predict pretty much what they're going to say next, but then they surprise you."

"Like when Laurie ran away."

"Yeah," he said heavily. "Like then. Why are you so interested in Laurie? You never even met her."

I explained about the book on Bobby's bookshelf. "I thought that was a pretty strange inscription on a book she gave to her stepbrother. What exactly do you think was going on between those two?"

Penn shrugged again. "I know Laurie's mom was really paranoid about Bobby. She thought he was a bad influence. When she figured out they were spending a lot of time together, she sort of freaked out and started spouting curfews and all kinds of restrictions. It was stupid."

"I can kind of see her mom's point of view, though."

Penn smiled. "Yeah, Bobby is kind of a mother's nightmare, isn't he? Mrs. J. hated it that Bobby was over at the house all the time."

"But I guess she couldn't do anything about it since he was coming to visit his dad."

"Right. The problem was Mrs. J. didn't seem to realize there wasn't anything she could do to stop Laurie from spending time with Bobby. She'd tell Laurie that Bobby wasn't allowed to come in when Laurie was there by herself, but how was she going to enforce it? Mrs. J. was hardly ever home, because the Jenkinses were trying to get a new printing business off the ground and they worked late practically every night. So Laurie went on doing what she wanted and Mrs. J. went on having fits."

"You aren't eating," I said, noticing that his donut was untouched.

He looked down at it. "I guess I'm not all that hungry."

"Do you think Bobby has heard from Laurie?"

"Don't ask me. Bobby and I don't even speak anymore." He smiled wanly. "Can we talk about something else? I know it's just interesting gossip to you, but for a friend of the runaway it's kind of a downer."

"I think I'm going to fail physics."

Penn's smile was brilliant. "Now, physics I can deal with. You don't have to fail physics. You don't have Mullins, do you?"

"No. I have Dockerty."

He looked relieved. "Good. Dockerty knows his stuff, at least. Bring your physics book along and I'll help you. If we can't do it, then Stephen can. He's really good at physics." Penn smiled. "That's the reason I came looking for you—"

"To help me with my physics?" I asked, confused.

"No, to ask you if you want to come out to my family's cabin on the river. We'll all be there, Tessa, Stephen, Casey. The bunch."

Suddenly I was afraid I wasn't going to be able to get the words out to accept. It was as if I had had a terrible attack of stage fright. I felt like an understudy who has just learned that the star has broken a leg. Can I do it? Will they like me? For a second that seemed like an eternity I sat in stupefied silence.

When I didn't answer at once, Penn looked worried. "You can bunk with Tessa," he added. "She usually brings the food. She's a terrific cook."

Then, as if a spell had been lifted by the anxiety I could hear in his voice, I spoke easily. "Should I bring anything?" I asked him.

"Just your own sweet self." Penn looked down at his hands self-consciously. "That's the kind of thing my mother always says. She says all these Old South kind of things like 'Goodness me' and 'Bless my heart' and 'Why, I've had a gracious plenty.'"

"She sounds nice."

"Well, yeah. She is. She's always been nice."

It occurred to me that Penn's little speech about how you never really know somebody might have more to do with his mother than with Laurie.

"Why don't I pick you up at about eight," he suggested. "It takes about a half hour to drive over there. It's nothing fancy, but it's got the basics. The weather report says it's supposed to warm up tomorrow, so maybe we can go tubing down the river. There's a place upstream where we can rent big inner tubes."

I was thinking how wonderful it would be not to be alone all weekend. Now I, too, had a place to go and friends to meet. I wasn't the pathetic kid who got left behind.

At the same time I was more than a little anxious. I'm not sure why, but all of a sudden I noticed that the woman in the last booth was crying. Her face was streaked with tears. The man reached over her table and touched her arm. I looked away from them hastily.

I was not going to worry about this weekend, I told myself. This was my chance to be with Penn, and I was going to enjoy it.

"We'll come back Sunday afternoon," Penn said.

"It sounds wonderful," I said, smiling at him warmly.

Ten

Dear Diary,

I've counted about a thousand sheep, but no luck. Just a few hours ago, when Penn invited me out to the cabin, I was faint from happiness, but now I'm only jittery. Not exactly excited-jittery, but nervous-jittery.

Laurie's face keeps getting in the way of the sheep. When I'm with Penn, I'm so distracted by him that I forget about Laurie, but later I wish he had told me something about her. I'm not sure what exactly, but something more. Because we're getting closer, right? Shouldn't he want to tell me more?

But now all I can think of is Laurie's messing up my sleep.

As I laid down my pen and closed my diary,

my flesh was clammy with anxiety. The name Laurie kept turning round and round in my head. What was it about her that bothered me? I had never even met her. Strange the way she had dropped suddenly out of sight like a pebble in a pond, leaving scarcely a trace. What had happened between her and Bobby? Perhaps they had a big falling-out before she left. That would explain it. Otherwise why would she have left without him? Maybe she had been desperate. I felt as if her face were covered in a mist. Some mystery clung to her. I had met her friends, her boyfriend, had seen her picture, but I had no feel at all for the kind of person she was and no explanation for why she had left town.

I was sure I wouldn't be able to sleep, so I went to the kitchen for a glass of warm milk. The plastic clock on the wall read 4:10. It whirred softly. The refrigerator rumbled, dropped a few ice cubes into the ice maker, and then fell silent. With a sudden feverish intensity I wanted to know that both Laurie and my mother, all those who were hurting and lost, were taken care of. My heart was pounding as if I were standing on the edge of a cliff.

The hot milk burned my tongue. Why was I worrying so much? Anxiety had infected me. These cold hours of the morning were when my fears sprang most vividly to life. Like faintly, crazily colored lights shining out of a projector, they took focus and form only when the shades were pulled and it grew dark.

I found the comic pages of the paper and read them. My head ached and I had the uneasy conviction that Mary Worth's new tenant was going to be a serial killer. I folded the paper and reluctantly went down the hall to my room.

As I slipped under the covers, it occurred to me that maybe my sleeplessness had to do with my anxiety about the weekend. More than anything, I wanted Penn and his friends to like me. The alternative was to be the invisible new girl, jealously observing other people's lives.

I closed my eyes and pictured myself painting a large number three. My arm is growing very heavy, I told myself.

In the morning Penn was a few minutes late picking me up. The sun was low and frosty looking, the trees in the yard cast long shadows, and the air smelled fresh. Dew streamed in bloodred rivulets down the hood of his Corvette. When he opened the trunk, I could see it was stuffed full of supplies for the weekend—a guitar case, boxes of large matches, bags of cookies and pretzels, batteries, books, and magazines.

The car, which had seemed too low the first time

I got in it, now seemed exactly right. I snuggled into the padded bucket seat, feeling more secure and comfortable than I had been in my own bed.

"It's not very far away," Penn said as we drove off. "The others are meeting us there. Wait till you see it!" His face lit up. "It's a different world. Out in the woods, on the river, completely away from it all."

He didn't seem to expect me to answer, and his low voice mingled with the sound of the engine and the whooshing wind outside. I fell to sleep almost immediately.

When the car stopped, I woke up and remembered my dream with a start. It was of Laurie Jenkins's face, as expressionless as if she were dead. Her mouth hung slightly open and her eyes had no pupils. Blood trickled down her face like sweat. My heart was still beating wildly. With a shock of relief I remembered the dew on Penn's car looking like blood. That was what had caused the bad dream. That was all it was. Simply the power of suggestion.

"We're here," Penn said softly.

I clasped my hands and stretched my arms before me. The uneasiness bred by the bad dream was falling away like fog before a rising sun. My legs felt useless. If I tried to stand up, I knew my knees would fold and I would collapse like a rag doll.

Penn opened the trunk and began tossing bags out on the ground. Outside the car windows, pine trees rose overhead, a canopy of green that let sunlight fall in spots on the dirt and dead leaves below. I got out of the car gingerly, feeling almost breathless, overcome with the quietness of the forest.

The cabin was a simply constructed A-frame at its front with a box of bedrooms added on. A bare pipe stuck up from the ground, spigot attached, not far from the car. It was left over, I later learned, from the days before a bathroom and sink had been installed inside. Wooden steps led to a landing and to the front door, which was painted red. Much of the house seemed to be glass, though a closer inspection showed that the bedrooms of the cottage were solidly enclosed with wood and it was only the living and dining room that was so spectacularly glassed in.

"Like it?" Penn asked.

"It's perfect."

"It's not very big," he said, in an unsuccessful attempt to sound modest. "My parents built it themselves stick by stick before I was born. I think they had a kit or something. Seems incredible, doesn't it?"

"It must have taken them forever."

"Years, I think. They used to call it 'the house that love built.' They came out here and camped under the stars until they got the roof on." He shifted his weight uncomfortably. "Well, I'd better get this stuff inside." He charged up the stairs.

Penn dropped the bags with a thud on the landing by the door and searched for his key. "What are you so serious about all of a sudden?" His eyes crinkled into amused triangles as he looked down at me.

"I'm having a sudden fit of *carpe diem*. You know, seize the day. Life is uncertain—eat dessert first." I hoisted a bag of groceries and followed him up the steps.

"You sound like Stephen. He says why worry about something that's not going to happen until he's thirty."

"All smokers say that."

"I guess. Of course, if he lives to be a hundred—"

"If you smoke, chances are you won't live to be a hundred."

"Good point. And if you'd been busy eating dessert the whole time, you'd be fat." He grinned, then picked up the bags, pushed the door open with his foot, and stepped inside. "It smells stale. We'd better open some windows."

Inside, the wood floors shone with wax. A fireplace decorated one wall of the living room. In front of it were some easy chairs and a couch with chintz covers in a soft, cabbage-rose print. On one side of the fireplace was a bookcase filled with books about snails and birds and spiders as well as a few tattered pieces of fiction and children's books. A counter separated the kitchen from the oblong wooden dining table. By the window over the stove were hung cooking pots, wire eggbeaters, and strainers. A handful of wooden spoons splayed out of a blue ceramic cup.

Penn threw open the kitchen window and the song of a mockingbird floated in.

"That bird is out of touch. It thinks it's spring," Penn said.

"Sometimes you can hear them singing at night, as if they're talking to themselves," I said. "Birds have a secret life. I'm sure of it."

"Why not?" said Penn. "All the rest of us do."

Penn glanced at me, but I could not speak. I was afraid my dark memories showed on my face.

Cutting his eyes away from me as if he sensed my discomfort and wanted to give me a moment of privacy, Penn gazed out the large expanse of glass that was the back side of the living area. "Usually you can see the river from here, but it's been such a dry year that the river is down. Sometimes I wonder if my mother misses this place—but I don't like to ask."

"You go to visit her?"

"Sure I go to visit her. It's not like she's dead."

"I know. I just hadn't thought about it."

"I'm the only one who comes out here now. Me and my friends. My dad never comes. I guess I'm the keeper of the flame." He smiled sadly.

I put the groceries on the kitchen counter and stood still a moment. Penn put his arms around my waist. His breath was warm on the nape of my neck and his nose tickled. "Your hair smells so clean," he murmured. "All last night I was worried you were going to back out of coming somehow. I kept thinking your house was going to be hit by a comet during the night, or your old boyfriend was going to show up from out of town. Even at the last minute, I kept thinking I'd walk up to your house and your father would be blocking the door."

"Any other worries?" I turned around to face him, laughing.

"Oh, sure. Lots of them." He grinned. "I just gave you the short list."

"Do you think the others will mind that I came?" I asked, a bit anxiously.

"Nah!" But his eyes shifted and I knew he was lying.

I wished Nikki Warren hadn't planted in my mind the idea that the group was unfriendly. It wasn't true, I told myself. They were only a little reserved. Even Casey hadn't been exactly hostile to me. Still, I couldn't persuade myself that any of them would be honestly glad to see me.

The sound of a car broke the forest silence, and a moment later Casey burst in the front door. "Hi," he panted.

"Hi," we chorused.

He dumped a couple of large cans of cranberry juice on the counter. "I forgot how far it was out here," he said. "I kept thinking I'd missed a turn. Wait'll you see what I've got."

He darted outside again and we could hear his footsteps thumping on the wooden stairs. A moment later he came in again with a small record player. "It runs on batteries," he explained proudly. He put it down on the low table that sat in front of the couch. "I guess they make them with batteries so people can use them in boats. Have you ever heard Edith Piaf? I can't believe I never heard her up till now. When everybody gets here, I'll play it. You've got to hear it." He rummaged around in a kitchen drawer for an opener, then poured out a tall glass of cranberry liquid. He seemed very much at home in the cabin. "This stuff is full of vitamins," he said, chugging it down. "I'll probably live forever."

"Yeah," Penn said lightly, "but why would anyone want to?"

Eleven

. . . I don't get it. The weekend had just started, and I thought we were having a really nice time. Then out of nowhere Penn says something so sad and morbid I feel he's a million miles away from me.

Why would Penn be tired of life when he has so much to live for? And what did he mean by that comment about everyone having a secret life? I wonder if he's trying to tell me something about the past—or the future—that I don't completely get.

Penn's sad smile plucked so painfully at my heart that I had to turn away.

Casey put down the glass. A cranberry-juice mustache showed on his upper lip, and he wiped his lips with the back of his arm. "I got a call from Mr. Hansen before I left," he said, scowling.

"The principal is calling you at home now?" Penn was surprised.

"Big problems. Somebody's sending the teachers obscene messages on the school computers."

"Casey has a part-time job managing the school's computer setup," Penn explained. "Actually, he even wrote a lot of the programs they use."

"Power!" Casey grinned. But his expression turned grim at once. "I wish I could find out who's behind it. They've got nerve, messing around with my computers."

"Probably just somebody fooling around," said Penn. "It's not like they're trying to get at you personally."

"Well, it's getting to me." Casey frowned. "If I could find out who was behind it, I'd scare those suckers to death. They'd be afraid to ever touch a computer again. If they want to send obscene messages, why don't they send them through the U.S. mail like everybody else? Why do they have to drag me into it? Mr. H. wants me to figure out how they get into the computers and try to stop them." He snorted scornfully. "He couldn't seem to catch on that there wasn't much I could do. I tried to explain to him that if you shut everybody out of the computer system, you might as well not have one, but the man's IQ is smaller than his shoe size." He looked around. "Where are Stephen and Tessa?"

"On their way," said Penn. "I guess they got off late."

A moment later the front door rattled. "I'll get it," I said.

When I opened the front door, Stephen and Tessa practically fell in. Their arms were full of grocery bags. "Hey," said Stephen.

"Hello, everyone," said Tessa. Without putting down the bags, she pecked Penn affectionately on the cheek. He took the paper bags from her and put one on the sofa. The bag tipped over, spilling books over the flowered chintz.

"Give me the groceries," said Tessa. She took the other bag from Penn, moved to the kitchen counter, and began fishing out fruit, vegetables, and bags of chips and cookies. She dumped out a bag of lemons, which wheeled and wobbled before coming to rest on the wooden counter. They looked, in the pool of light from the window, like a still-life painting of lemons, too perfect to be real.

Stephen put a dozen eggs and a six-pack of soda into the refrigerator.

"I promised Joanna we'll help her with physics," said Penn.

Stephen groaned. "That's all I need. More physics. Hey, I've got an idea! Somebody ought to call up the police—anonymously, of course—and charge Dockerty with child abuse. Good idea, or what?"

"Listen up, you guys. You gotta hear this." Casey fiddled with the phonograph and a scratchy warble floated through the air. *"Je ne regrette rien. Je—Je ne regrette rien."*

"What's that?" cried Stephen. "Where's that coming from?"

Casey and Tessa spoke at the same time. "It's the record player," said Tessa.

"It's French," said Casey. "Don't you love her voice? She's neat."

"Your way with words always awes us, Casey," Tessa said coldly.

"I regret nothing," I translated.

"Probably a lie," muttered Penn.

"It's an old record, that's why it sounds scratchy," Casey explained. "I found it in the garage. Can you imagine putting something so cool in the garage? Lucky thing it didn't get mildewed."

Somehow I was surprised to find that a computer freak like Casey had a passion for a dead French singer. When that song was over, something gloomy about the simple and sad life of country folk started to play. I was barely listening anymore, because Penn's fingers touched mine and it was hard for me to think straight for a moment. His light-colored eyes stared into mine. In the clear light of the cabin and standing so close to him, I could see there was actually a thin rim of brown around the black pupil that made the dark center look larger than it was. Shooting out from it were rays of light blue, faint gray, and pale green. I smiled at him, feeling foolish but unable to help myself.

"That song's dumb," said Casey, impatiently lifting the needle. "*Je ne regrette rien*," the record began again.

Stephen froze. "How many times are you going to play that thing?"

"Don't you like it?" Casey asked innocently. "It's a great song."

"It looks like really good weather," put in Tessa quickly. "We're not going to get many days as nice as this before spring. I say we should go upstream and rent tubes."

"I didn't bring a swimsuit," I said, suddenly in a panic.

"Wear jeans. That's what I'm going to do," said Tessa.

"Don't forget the cooler," cried Casey. "We can tie the cooler to a tube and then we'll have drinks all the way down the river. Do you still have that Styrofoam cooler, Penn?"

"It's not all that warm," said Tessa. "We won't need any drinks. Let's just do it."

Casey lifted the needle and began the song again. "Isn't that something?" he asked. "I love it."

Stephen took a sudden step toward Casey, but Tessa restrained him with a hand on his chest. "Casey, not everybody has your iron nerves. Could you please stop playing that thing over and over? Come on, let's get out of here."

There was a good bit of discussion about whether the bait shop upstream would have inner tubes available to rent, considering the season, but in the end we decided to give it a try. We took two cars. The plan was to leave one car downstream to use to ride back to the bait shop when we had had enough of tubing. Penn and I piled in with Tessa and Stephen, and Casey went in his rattletrap green Plymouth, since the Corvette was not practical for transporting groups of people.

It felt odd to be in the backseat of Stephen's car again, but this time pressed close to Penn and with his smell mingled with the dark, smoky scent of the car. It seemed as if a long time had passed since I'd last been in that back-seat—so much had happened since then. I looked down at Penn's fingers wrapped around my hand. This is it! I thought. This is what I have been waiting for.

"Casey is being a royal pain," Stephen said, his teeth clenched. "He knows he's getting to me, and he's doing it on purpose."

Tessa shot me an uneasy smile. "We could stand to be a teensy bit more laid back, couldn't we?"

Stephen growled and showed his even white teeth, then snapped them closed with a click.

"Down, tiger." Tessa stroked his hair. "Casey doesn't realize how much he gets on people's nerves."

"Joanna says he does," said Penn, "and that he does it on purpose."

"That's what I said!" cried Stephen. "See—Joanna agrees with me. That's proof. I've got an impartial witness."

"We need to make sure Casey feels appreciated," said Tessa, her voice soothing. "He has a very strong need to feel important."

"So what?" said Stephen. "I'm insecure. You're insecure. Penn's insecure. I don't know Joanna very well yet, but my guess is she's insecure, too, and none of the rest of us go playing a stupid record over and over again until—" He flipped his hair back with a restless toss of his head. "It would get to anybody."

Casey's car pulled off the road ahead of us

and Stephen stopped his car behind it.

"Is this far enough from the bait place?" Casey shouted to us. "Too far? What do you think?"

"It looks about right to me," Penn said. "Get in, Casey."

Casey squeezed into the backseat with Penn and me. "This bunch is starting to feel like Noah's ark," he grumbled. "Everybody's in pairs. I'm going to have to get me a girl if this keeps up."

"I don't see things like that," said Tessa. "Do you, Penn? Stephen? Just a bunch of friends together, that's how I see it."

"It's not like you haven't had girlfriends," said Stephen. "Whatever happened to Bitsy Whoosis?"

"Bitsy Whalen," said Tessa helpfully.

"No looks, no brains," pronounced Casey. "She thinks calculus is something you scrape off the shower walls."

"What *is* the stuff you scrape off the shower walls?" asked Stephen.

"Yuck," said Tessa.

"Is that the technical term?" Stephen asked.

"Besides," said Casey, ignoring him, "I'm looking for a more womanly-type woman." He outlined an hourglass shape with his hands.

I tried to get as far away from Casey as the

backseat would allow. I hadn't been around such a sexist pig since the seventh grade.

The bait shop was not much more than a large shack. The place was decorated with peeling paint and a rusty Coca-Cola sign. Large shallow boxes of dirt raised up off the ground with cement blocks stood to one side of the shack. "That's where they keep the worms," Tessa explained. "The minnows and crayfish are in those metal barrels by the front door. I keep wondering about what they eat." She licked her lips and looked vaguely green.

"Are you okay?" I asked, moving toward her.

She smiled unsteadily. "I'm fine." She turned abruptly and moved away swiftly to catch up with the others.

I stared for a moment at the barrels of crayfish and thought of bodies thrown in the river, murdered bodies fetched up and found, upon autopsy, to have bullets in the brain. The fingers of the corpse are only slightly nibbled by crayfish and crabs.

Swearing under my breath, I rushed to catch up with Tessa. I was letting my wild imagination get out of hand, I told myself firmly. It was one of those odd little moments that I was to remember later as almost psychic—as if I already knew of the terrible things that were going to happen.

*   *   *

On the porch of the bait shop was a pile of fat inner tubes, each one with a number painted on it. The shop's owner, who smelled strongly of fish and tobacco, rented us the tubes for the afternoon. We locked our shoes and wallets in the car, rolled up our jeans, waded out into the water, and leapt onto the inner tubes.

"Ouch!" cried Tessa. "It's cold!"

"You'll get used to it," said Casey, his teeth chattering.

The sun shed its thin warmth on our faces and arms. The real problem turned out to be not the chilly water, but the rocks. The water of the river was so low that we were constantly scraping on the rocky bottom of the riverbed. Although there were one or two places the tubes actually floated, for the most part we had to scoot along over the rocks by pushing ourselves forward with our hands.

The folded cuffs of my jeans were like ice around my knees. My rear, which had sunk into the hole of the inner tube, was quickly losing all sensation in the cold. My underpants itched and felt glued to me.

After a while Penn said, "I give up," and stood up suddenly. He was midcalf deep in the shallow water. "Let's walk back."

We all sprang up out of the inner tubes at once, as if on command. The seats of our jeans sagged heavily and cold water streamed down our legs. Picking our way carefully over the rocks, we scrambled up the riverbank, our toes sinking into the mud. Fat inner tubes wobbling awkwardly over our arms, we walked back to the bait shop.

The proprietor sat in a rocking chair watching us with amusement. His left cheek bulged with a wad of chewing tobacco. "Y'all giving up already?"

Stephen shook his head. "The river's too low."

The man spit a stream of brown juice into an empty soup can, then carefully put the can back in its place on the porch railing. "It's been a dry winter," said the man. "Can't recall a drier one."

"We'll have to try again in the summer," said Penn, smiling. Ordinary courtesy was a habit with him. I thought about how he had told me his mother was always nice. He was a lot like that himself. "We'll take some firewood while we're here," he said.

We loaded the firewood into the trunk of the car, each of us carrying a few pieces at a time.

"That guy knew the river was too dry to tube down," Casey complained as we got in the car. "We ought to have demanded a refund."

Penn gave him a look.

"Okay," said Casey crossly, "*you* ought to have demanded a refund."

I hadn't noticed until then that Penn had paid for Casey's inner tube. It cost only a couple of dollars, and I had taken the money out of my wallet and paid it without thinking. I wondered if Casey's family had suffered some terrible financial misfortune, and that was why Penn had paid his share. Maybe Casey had a really good reason for being such a jerk, and that was why the others were patient with him.

After we dropped Casey off where he had left his car, we sped back to the cabin. "What does Casey's father do for a living?" I asked.

"He's some kind of business consultant," said Tessa vaguely. "He flies all over the place. Casey's mom is a social worker, which sort of makes you think, doesn't it?"

"What does it make you think?" I had reluctantly concluded that it was unlikely Casey's family was poor.

"I mean, you can hardly find anybody less politically correct than Casey," said Tessa. "You heard him on women. He's a pig."

"If you get him started, he can be pretty bad," Stephen agreed.

I resolved not to get him started. As far as I was concerned, Casey was hard enough to take when he was being pleasant.

When we got back to the cabin, we all changed into dry clothes and hung our jeans on the railing of the landing. In the feeble warmth we were getting from the January sky, I figured it would probably take about six months for them to dry. Once we were inside, Stephen and Tessa, to my surprise, pulled out paper and pencil and began helping me tackle physics. Tessa was patient and could generally see what it was I found so mysterious about the problem. Stephen's mind was quick and solved the questions in flashes like lightning. He saw connections, made analogies, and even thought up rhymes to help me remember rules. They took on my work as if it were their own without a trace of impatience. Paper covered with formulas began to litter the floor, and the pages of my physics book were getting soft and dog-eared from use. My back hurt and I felt guilty that they were spending their weekend helping me. "I really appreciate this, you guys," I said.

"It's good for us, isn't it, Tess?" Stephen asked.

"Oh, absolutely," Tessa agreed. "We like doing it."

"It helps us get a better grasp on the stuff ourselves." Stephen gave me a smile of such sweetness that I could see why Tessa loved him.

Later we all walked along a path in the

woods, balancing on rotting fallen logs, stepping over muddy rivulets. The path was ferny, mossy, and padded with mats of dead leaves and pine needles. Wading in a cold, shallow stream, we caught salamanders in our hands. No bigger than minnows, they were colorless and wiggly. It was unsettling to feel the creature alive in my palms, and I quickly let mine slip away. At once it became invisible in the water.

Casey knew the names of the trees. "Casey's better than a botany book," Tessa said. "We're so lucky."

We returned to the cabin, tired, and flopped down on the sofa and chairs. Stephen, Tessa, and Casey got out cards and played hearts. I noticed Casey was cheating, but it never occurred to me to mention it. I was feeling my sleepless night by then and was giddy and a little disoriented. I leafed through a children's book I found on the shelf, *Honeybunch Goes to Summer Camp*. I was up to chapter five—Honeybunch had learned how to make a camp shower out of a pierced tin can—when I realized I was longing for a hot bath. Not a shower out of a tin can, but a steaming bath with masses of warm bubbles. But getting up to take a bath took more energy than I could summon. I broke open a cellophane bag and ate a hard chocolate-chip cookie. Casey put on Edith Piaf again. *"Je ne regrette rien"* pierced the air.

"Can't you play some other song, Casey?" Penn asked, his voice carefully even.

"But this is the *best* one," Casey insisted. "Don't you guys like music?"

Penn laid aside his book. "I'm hungry," he said. "Let's eat. Can we help, Tessa?"

"You know how Tessa gets crazy if you mess with her while she's cooking," Stephen said.

"It's no problem." Tessa leapt up. "I'll throw on a few simple things. Give me twenty minutes. You guys wash the salad greens."

"What fun," Stephen said.

Tessa swatted him playfully.

Tessa's meal turned out to be a feast. When we had finished, Casey patted his flat stomach and said, "That was as good as sex with a nymphomaniac. I think we'll keep you, Tessa."

Tessa's eyes met mine in a pointed look.

I helped her clear the table. Penn and Stephen, as if anxious to disassociate themselves from Casey, leapt up from their chairs and began washing up and scrubbing pots and pans. They even scoured the stove. Over the clatter, I heard Casey's record player. He seemed to be determined to drive Stephen crazy.

Twelve

. . . Not even Casey—who, by the way, is doubly irritating when you're trapped inside a cabin with him—can spoil this moment. (No, I won't start wondering why, why, why they hang out with him. It seems that every time I get an answer I'm wrong anyway, so I might as well have happier thoughts and stare at Penn.) . . .

After dinner we gathered around the hearth as the fire painted leaping patterns of light and darkness on the sofa and cast long shadows into the kitchen. The glass of the living-room walls looked black, as if the forest outside had disappeared.

I took out my diary and began to write.

Today at Penn's cabin I felt my life click-

123

*ing into place for the first time. I know that
there is something perfect for me about this
crowd, about Penn and this place.*

Casey stretched out full length on the couch,
crunching a cookie. Stephen was sunk into one
overstuffed chair, a leg hooked over one arm.
Tessa sat on the other, a stainless-steel bowl in
her lap, snapping green beans. I sat cross-legged,
leaning against the couch, writing. Penn lay on
his stomach, propped up with his arms, watching
the flames as if hypnotized.

My pen hesitated. "I wish we could stay here
forever," I said.

"What?" Tessa's cheeks dimpled. "And give
up our big ambitions?"

"What's your big ambition?" I asked.

"Well, first, Princeton, of course."

"Tessa's dad went there, so she's a legacy,"
Stephen said gloomily. "She's a sure admit."

"I have my heart set on it," admitted Tessa.
"I know they tell you not to get set on one college, but my dad took me up to look at it a
couple of years ago and I was a goner. I hope I
get in."

"You will," said Stephen.

"And then I want to write cookbooks, become famous, and have wonderful children and
give brilliant dinner parties where major world

issues are settled between the chocolate mousse and the coffee!"

"I have got to get into Princeton." Stephen gritted his teeth.

"It'll all work out," cooed Tessa. "Don't worry about it so much."

"Stephen is a National Merit Finalist." Penn smiled. "Does my father ever wish he had that kind of material to work with."

"Yeah, like your scores are a disaster or something," said Stephen.

"Penn's dad wants him to be a doctor," put in Casey.

"What would you do if it were up to you?" I asked Penn.

"Oh, he'd be a nurse or an orderly or a medical technician," said Tessa, her eyes mischievous. "Penn has a very strong stomach. He can do all of that kind of stuff. When we were dissecting a cat in class, I thought I was going to retch, but Penn was great. We all used to stand back and let him do his stuff. He absolutely loved cutting through those formaldehyde-stiff muscles." She shuddered.

"It was interesting," Penn countered. "Every day, something exciting. Now, the liver! That was a day!" He smiled.

"You are strange," Tessa teased. "Look how his eyes start to mist over when he talks about the liver!"

I was puzzled. "I don't get it. If you're actually interested in medicine and your dad is willing to pay to send you to med school, why not go ahead and be a doctor?"

"I wouldn't give him the satisfaction," Penn said. He scrambled up and with his back to us began poking the fire.

"And of course, Casey's hoping to get accepted at MIT," said Tessa. "But even if he gets in, he probably won't graduate, because he'll drop out to make his first million."

"You know, Casey, you'd better brace yourself. At MIT you're going to run into a lot of people smarter than you are," said Stephen.

"No way!" cried Casey indignantly.

"But none will have more self-confidence," added Tessa. "And I, for one, will always ask you to my brilliant dinner parties, Casey, dear, no matter."

Casey snorted. "Like I'm losing sleep over whether I get asked to dinner parties. Get rich enough and you never have to worry. You'll have plenty of friends and more dinner parties than you know what to do with."

"Sure," Stephen said. "You can always buy those friends, right?"

"What about you, Joanna?" Tessa asked. "What's your big ambition?"

"Just to stay out of jail." I shrugged. An awkward silence fell, and I saw Stephen and Tessa look at each other. Hot color rose to my face. "What I mean," I went on quickly, "is that I guess I'll muddle through somehow or other. I've got my applications in at a few state schools and I guess I haven't thought about it much beyond that."

"Why bother?" Casey asked. "Since you're a girl, you'll probably just get married anyway."

"No, I won't," I said. "Marriage is the biggest rip-off of the century. A white lace dress, flowers, the reception and all the attendants—it's a con. You get to be the center of attention for one day and it's supposed to convince you marriage is the start of something wonderful, but all it means is two strangers start living together. Pretty soon a squalling red-faced baby makes stranger number three and none of them ever gets a decent night's sleep again."

"Phew. That's a bleak view," said Penn. He was pale and his eyes were fixed on the floor.

"You've had a bad experience," said Tessa softly. "Marriage isn't always like that."

"My parents are still married." Stephen managed a faint smile. "So are Tessa's. They seem pretty happy."

Penn was sitting on his haunches now, stirring the fire. His face reflected the warmth of the flames and his hair was ruffled by the draft of air rushing into the chimney. "I think it would be nice to have a family."

"You don't need a family, Penn," said Tessa promptly. "You've got us."

The wind whistled the top of the chimney, making the fire leap. Penn tilted his head and stared at the flames, listening. I could hear it now myself, the wind in the trees, like a long sigh. "The weather's changing," he said. "Hear?"

Casey craned his neck to read over my shoulder. "Get a load of this, you guys! Joanna's not writing in English!"

"You keep your journal in French?" Stephen asked, looking interested. "I've thought about doing that."

"No! It's not French," said Casey. "It's jabberwocky. It doesn't even have any vowels."

I closed my diary, blushing.

"I've got it. The lady is—Hungarian!" cried Tessa. "And what's more—she's of royal blood."

"Leave Joanna alone," Penn ordered.

"Seriously," said Stephen, "what language are you using?"

"It's code," I admitted.

They all looked at me blankly.

"She's a spy," said Casey. "I knew it. Watch what you say around her."

"It's a habit with me now," I said, conscious of

my burning face. "I've done it for years. It's a stupid, simple code. I made it up myself, and now I use it all the time and don't even think about it."

"Could I figure it out?" asked Penn. I let him take my diary from my hands.

"Better not!" warned Stephen. "You might find out something you don't want to know."

Penn stared at a page. "No danger," he said. "I can't understand a word of it."

"I bet I could crack it," said Casey. "Give it here."

"Stop it, Casey," said Tessa. "You don't like people breaking into your computers, do you? It's the same thing. Give Joanna some space or she might clobber you."

"Yes, well, you'd know all about that, wouldn't you?" Casey said, but he stretched out again on the couch.

I took the diary from Penn and stuffed it into my duffel bag. "It's just everyday observations, my impressions, things like that. Pretty dull stuff."

"I never heard of anybody keeping a diary in code," said Casey. "It makes you kind of wonder." He gazed at me speculatively.

"Oh, come on," said Tessa. "You said yourself, Casey, that you're interested in codes. Why are you getting on Joanna for making one up? It's, like, a hobby."

"It *is* like a hobby," I said gratefully. "I've done it for ages. I write pages and pages of stuff. It helps me make sense out of things."

"Maybe I should take it up," Penn said dryly. "Nothing much makes sense to me anymore."

"I've never kept a diary," said Casey.

"Yeah, but that's because you're practically illiterate," said Stephen.

"Have *you* ever kept a diary?" Casey asked challengingly. "Only girls write diaries. They write in these fat curly letters with hearts over the *i*'s, they lock them with this little lock you can pick with a paper clip, and all they write about is who likes them and who doesn't like them. It's a complete waste of time."

"One would almost think you had picked the lock of your sister's diary," said Tessa.

Casey laughed. "Sure. I did. But bo-ring! I couldn't get into it at all."

"That's because it was written in a sneaky code, like Joanna's," said Tessa. "Probably every time you read 'I think Richard likes me,' it really meant 'Casey is a poo-poo head.'"

"Very funny," said Casey sourly. "Like my little sister is really into codes in the sixth grade."

"That's when I started with mine," I said.

Penn was pulling a box from under the couch. "Anybody for Scrabble?"

"Watch out, Joanna. For Penn, Scrabble is a blood sport," said Stephen.

"Not this time, I promise. This game's for fun," said Penn.

"Catch the gleam in his eye," teased Tessa.

I am normally a demon Scrabble player myself, but whether it was the hypnotic spell of the fire or the way Penn's eyes kept meeting mine, the game was less competitive than dreamy. I found myself playing words because they looked like fun.

Stephen added "qua" to "king" to make "quaking" on a triple word score, but Penn and I only looked at each other and laughed.

"Penn is off his game," said Casey, who wasn't playing. "Maybe I'll put on a record. Wake us all up."

"Casey!" snapped Tessa. "Don't!"

"Maybe we ought to go to bed," said Penn, getting up. "I'm beat."

"That's right. Call off the game when I'm sixty points ahead," Stephen argued, but he yawned.

I could hear the wind, louder now, in the tall trees outside. It was cold when I stepped away from the fire. The weather was changing. I had written much of the evening in my diary, and already it seemed like a sweet memory. The shadows cast by the fire danced on the ceiling, shifting and changing until the walls of the house seemed like a moving veil swaying in the breeze. I was so tired I was dizzy, and the light from the fire was disorienting. I was wobbly on my feet from having sat cross-legged so long, and I grabbed the back of the couch to steady myself.

"Joanna's about to pass out," said Penn. "We should have gone to bed an hour ago."

Tessa kissed Stephen good night, and I followed her into the first room, with its narrow twin beds. After the lazy heat of the fire, the air in the room hit me like a cold shower, though its door had been left open and the heat of the fire had made it the warmest of the three bedrooms.

Too tired now to even think of a bath, I unzipped my bag and got into my pajamas. I was surprised to see, when Tessa stripped, that she had a trim, perfect figure. Without realizing it, I had expected her to look melted and sloppy to match her clothes. One dim lamp shed a feeble orangish light into the room, but it did not reach the corners, which were full of shadows. The beds had been casually made up, with patchwork quilts pulled up over the pillows.

I lifted the edge of the quilt and sat on the bed.

"Watch it as you get in," warned Tessa. "Sometimes mice get in the house in the winter. I put on a shoe too quick one morning and I felt something furry in the toe."

I cautiously slid under the covers, and almost at once my toe encountered something fuzzy. I leapt out, both feet on the wood floor in no time. My teeth were chattering. "I felt something."

"Throw back the quilt," suggested Tessa. "That ought to scare it away."

I was not eager to have a mouse scampering over my toes and stood there frozen with indecision.

Tessa bravely flipped back the covers, revealing a rolled-up sock.

"Oh, no." Her arms fell to her sides and she stared at it in horror.

"It's only a sock," I said.

"L-Laurie's sock," Tessa stuttered. Then she seemed to recover. "She always wore socks to bed. She claimed she had the coldest feet in the world."

"And she didn't?"

"I don't know. I never slept with her."

I blinked.

Tessa got under her own covers, her teeth chattering. "We should leave the door open, to get whatever heat is left from the fire," she said. "It's definitely turning colder outside."

"Okay," I agreed, although the leaping shadows from the fire made the room seem even more eerie. I tossed the sock under the bed and pulled the quilt up to my chin. "Have you heard from Laurie since she ran away?" I asked.

"No." Tessa was silent a moment. "She's written her mom, though. That's what I hear. To say she's all right."

"Nobody knows why she left?"

"Her mother is sure she's pregnant," said Tessa. "Mrs. J. thinks she skipped out so she wouldn't have to face the inevitable disapproval at home."

Remembering the passionate inscription in the book she gave to Bobby, I thought it seemed like a plausible explanation. "Do you think that's right?"

"Not really. Mrs. J. just doesn't want to believe Laurie would skip town to get away from her, that's all. Everybody else finds that pretty easy to believe—Mrs. J. is a horror."

"I heard you and Laurie were good friends."

Tessa's head turned toward me. I could see the pale oval of her face faintly in the dim, flickering light. "Who told you that?" she asked.

"Oh, Nikki, I guess. Was she wrong?"

"We ran around together. We had a lot of good times. But looking back—I don't know. Laurie was very reserved. I guess I didn't know that much about what was going on with her, really."

That much is obvious, I thought.

"Penn didn't have anything going with Laurie, did he?" I asked, a bit anxiously.

"Oh, no!" Tessa's answer was reassuringly prompt. "They were friends, that's all. I mean, Laurie was somebody who'd always been around, like Casey. I know this is hard to believe, but in first grade, we were all in the same reading group, and then later on Penn and Casey always went to the same summer camp, and Laurie and I went to Camp Cheerio for three years running. I don't know—people get to be part of your life. It's hard to figure out how it happens."

"You mean, and then you find out you don't really know them that well at all? Is that what you're getting at?"

"I guess. I'm not sure. I certainly know Stephen. And Penn. And Casey." She paused. "I guess I thought I knew Laurie, too. I don't know. I'm too tired to figure all this out." She rolled over, putting an end to the conversation.

I no longer cared if I was filling in Laurie's slot and sleeping in the bed where she had carelessly left a fuzzy sock. I sat up in bed and groped for my diary. Taking out the pen that was folded inside it, I began to write by the flickering light of the fire.

Thirteen

Dear Diary,

I don't know what to think. According to everyone, Laurie was such good friends with the group, but Tessa seems oddly cold when she talks about her.

Laurie was fool enough to run away from all this. I won't be so stupid. This happiness is all I ever wanted out of life. I love this place, the smell of the fire, the flickering of the shadows, the cold clean air that stings my nostrils when I take a deep breath in this little bedroom. I can feel the peace of the place seeping into my blood and pulsing in my veins.

I feel that by asking me to come along, Penn has given this place to me—he wants me here. He needs me. How I can *be sure of that, I don't know, but I am.*

At nine o'clock, when Tessa and I got out of bed, I could hear the steady sound of rain falling outside the window. Gloom had gathered under the pine trees outside. The half-open door was a slim rectangle of light showing that someone was up already. A shower was running, and Penn was banging on a door. "Casey!" he yelled. "Don't use up all the hot water. There are four other people here, remember?"

Casey's voice began warbling, "*Je ne regrette rien.*"

Tessa and I found Stephen in the kitchen measuring coffee into the coffee maker. "Morning." He kissed Tessa on the lips, then put his arms around her and kissed her again. "Mmm. You taste good. I might have to eat you."

"Casey's going to use all the hot water," Penn said gloomily. "He's pretending he doesn't hear me."

Tessa and Stephen sighed in unison, then began energetically opening and closing drawers, taking out pots and pans, eggs, bacon. They set Penn to work grating cheese, but one look apparently convinced them I wouldn't be of much use. I ate a slice of dry toast and stared glumly at the empty table, trying to quell the queasy feeling in my stomach. I am not at my best in the morning.

I could hear the clink of silverware and smell the bacon spitting in a skillet. Just as Casey emerged from the bathroom in a cloud of steam, breakfast appeared on the table—hot Danishes, crisp bacon, scrambled eggs with cheese. The sight and smell of so much food early in the morning was more than I could cope with.

Casey, barefoot and in jeans, sat down at the head of the table as if the meal had been prepared for him. He was pink as a lobster from his long stay under the hot shower, and his face clashed with his orange hair.

"Didn't you hear me telling you to take it easy on the hot water?" Penn asked.

Casey spread a napkin on his lap. "Nah. The shower makes such a racket in there, and I was singing."

"That better be the last time I hear that song," Stephen said icily.

"Somebody hasn't had his morning coffee," said Casey, buttering his toast. "Somebody who shall be nameless is pretty nasty in the morning. Ever had trouble with that temper of yours, Stephen?"

Stephen went white; he looked as if Casey had stabbed him in the stomach. I felt a quick sympathy for Stephen. I had suffered, too, from

Casey's sadistic probing. But at the same time I was curious. What could Casey be talking about? All I had seen of Stephen was patience and extraordinary sweetness. Even the story that Nikki had told featured Tessa's losing her temper, not Stephen. I found myself thinking how little I really knew about them.

I was glad to leave the table and get away from the heavy platters of food. I took my clothes into the bathroom and washed in cold water, saving the small amount of warm water remaining in the shower for washing my hair. I came out shivering, my wet hair streaming down the nape of my neck.

After my shower, I washed dishes while the others took turns in the shower. Soon we were ready to leave and began packing the cars. As we worked, water dribbled from the trees and mist was cold on our faces. Everything we touched was sticky and damp. We tracked pine needles into the house and dropped our belongings in the mud in our hurry to pitch our luggage in the car and get out of the damp. At last, though, we were loaded up, and Penn locked the front door of the cabin with a final click of the key.

Rain was coming down in sheets as we drove away. I could hear it drumming on the roof and rushing under our tires. Soon it was driving against the windshield with such a blinding force that I had the sensation we were underwater. Suddenly the red taillights of a truck glowed at us through the streaming windshield. Catching my breath, I remembered stories I had heard of sports cars being sucked under trucks.

Penn's blinker light clicked—he was going to try to pass. I was afraid to look at the speedometer, because we had already been going over the speed limit when we came up behind the truck. Instead I focused on the two solid lines I could barely make out in the middle of the road, solid lines that we were gobbling up under our wheels. The side windows were fogged and I couldn't tell much about where we were, but clearly we were in a no-passing zone. My shoulder was pressed against the door as the car veered into the left lane. Then I saw Penn's knuckles whiten and I felt us skating sideways. The truck roared and pulled ahead. I was breathless in terror as I felt our car spin, caught in the winds of the big truck's wake. All traction lost, we skated crazily until suddenly we slid to a stop.

The Corvette's red snout had come to rest not six inches from the steel guardrail. Rain drummed on the car like static. The lights of the car shone on the guardrail for several seconds before Penn turned to look at me. Neither of us spoke. I guess we were in shock.

At last Tessa's face appeared at Penn's window, a ghostly version of itself through the fogged window. Penn rolled the window down and I was hit by ricocheting drops. The rain was still coming down full force, and water streamed down Tessa's face. Her eyelashes stuck together in wet points and hair was plastered in odd-looking wisps to her forehead. "Are you two okay?" she shrieked over the noise of the pounding rain.

I nodded mutely, not at all sure I could speak.

"What is it going to take to make you slow down, Penn?" she screamed. "Are you out of your mind? Is this some kind of death wish? I wish you'd explain it to me. If you're plain-out insane, tell us now."

Stephen put his hand on her shoulder and, as if calmed by his touch, Tessa stopped shouting. She stood there breathing through her mouth, pale and angry. Stephen was holding a newspaper over his head to shield his head from the rain. His shirt was flesh-colored where it stuck to him. "We're just glad you're okay. You *are* okay, aren't you?"

Penn made a helpless gesture with one hand. "Sure." He licked his lips, and I realized they were bleached as pale as his skin. "We're fine." His voice was hoarse.

"You're okay to drive?" Stephen peered at Penn.

"Yeah. I'm okay," said Penn more firmly.

"Okay, good. Maybe we can slow down some now," said Stephen, "so we can all get home in one piece. You'd better get back on the road before another truck comes along. Nobody can see three yards out here the way it's coming down. The next thing you know, we're all going to end up pasted to the road like frogs." He held the newspaper over Tessa's head and they disappeared into the rain.

I rubbed a clear circle on my frosted window and looked out. Penn got the car back on the road. When I next looked at the speedometer, he was driving well under the legal limit. Neither of us said anything for quite a while. He brushed his hair out of his eyes. Finally he said softly, "I'm sorry."

"It's all right."

"No, it's not all right. It was stupid. I almost got us killed, and I just want you to know I'm going to do better."

Our near brush with death should have given me a lot to think about. But just after our narrow escape, I don't believe I thought anything. I was simply weak with relief.

We drove up into my driveway, next to my parked car. Penn turned off the windshield wipers. "I'm really glad you came along," he said, his eyes meeting mine.

"I'm glad, too. It was fun." I caught my breath. Should I say it was the best weekend of my life? Should I tell him I wanted to move to the cabin and live there with him forever, because I had never been so happy? "A lot of fun," I added.

He bent toward me until my nose rested on his cheek. "Your nose is cold," he said, pinching it gently between his fingers. Then his nose nuzzled mine, playfully, until finally his lips pressed against mine. I felt his fingers warm on my cheek. Then his tongue softly touched mine and warmth spread through me until I was conscious only of a slow pulsing happiness. "Mmm." He drew away and looked at me with a small smile.

I swallowed and licked my lips self-consciously. "I'd better go on in."

"Nah, let's stay here forever."

I laughed. "No, really." I gave him a peck on the cheek and threw the car door open, not giving myself time to think better of it. Rain hit me in the face. "It's pouring!"

Penn ran around to the trunk and threw it open. He hoisted my duffel over his shoulder as I groped for the house key. "Don't slip on the steps," he yelled as we ran up to the front door.

He tossed the duffel bag in the open door,

stepped inside after me, lifted me off the floor, put his arms around me, and kissed me. I was so wet, my shoes made a sucking noise when he lifted me up. "I could do this all day," Penn said.

"Except that we've got to get into dry clothes and do our homework."

"Crushed again. Look, I'll call you."

I watched him run to his car and jump in. He rolled down the window and waved. Then his tires squealed and he drove away with a roar into the rain.

When I woke up Monday morning, I could hear my father's snores in the next bedroom. I peeked in his room and saw him lying there, his arms flung back toward the bedposts. A loud snore rattled the room, and the hairs of his mustache were ruffled by his breath. His face was flushed. I closed the door silently and slipped out of the house.

Outside the sky was dark with low-lying black clouds. At school a big stack of the student newspaper had been left at the entrance to Eastman. Kids were there picking up copies and milling around in the passageway, catching up on the news. The air smelled damp. Little gusts of wind rustled the newspapers and made the boys' windbreaker jackets billow out behind them like sails. Wet sneakers squeaked on the smooth cement.

I was perched on the brick wall of Eastman with Penn, Casey, Tessa, and Stephen. The five of us were talking among ourselves in low voices. Maybe it was the way that the bunch had of withdrawing a little that made Nikki call us unfriendly, I thought. I could make out Nikki's characteristic croak amid the low chatter around us. "I talked to his girlfriend last night," she was saying. "She's okay—a few cuts and bruises. But they're treating him for head injuries. He was wearing a seat belt, but his head hit the steering wheel. Lucky thing somebody saw them crash! They could have been trapped in the car for hours. This time of year hardly anybody goes up to Lookout Point."

Every word Nikki spoke hammered into my brain. It could have been Penn and me who ended up in the hospital.

I was startled when one of the kids picking up a newspaper spoke to us. "Hey, Stephen," said the boy. "Isn't Lookout Point where you guys go hiking? I mean, don't you have more or less permanent dibs on that picnic table up there? I've heard about all the fancy lunches, man. I wish you'd invite me."

"Forget it, Mike," said his neighbor. "Coach told you to lose weight."

"We haven't been up there lately," said Stephen.

"No kidding?" said Mike, in evident surprise. "I thought you guys were always up there."

"No, not really." Stephen sounded wary. "We go out to Penn's cabin more these days."

"I've never been to Lookout Point," I said. "Is it nice?"

"You get a view of the falls from there," Nikki volunteered, turning her round face toward me. "But actually the postcard view is from the ground, not the overlook. I mean, what's the point of looking at falls from the top? It's from below you get the foam and stuff. You ought to go out there, Joanna. It's a tourist sight."

"The falls haven't run for months," said Penn, "because of the drought."

"Some drought," said a blond girl, peering anxiously at the gray sky. "The river's going to flood if this keeps up."

The bell for first period rang, and I slipped down from the wall. I was reluctant to leave the others, even though we would be meeting again in a few hours for lunch. It was the first and breathless stage of our friendship, and everything we did together was, for me at least, incredibly exciting. I was impressed with Casey's brilliance and charmed by Stephen and Tessa's passion. And then there was Penn. I had never been so attracted to a guy in my life.

When I got to homeroom, an announcement crackled over the intercom. "All seniors applying to State or to Chapel Hill should come to the gym at once to meet with campus representatives."

Virtually every kid in my homeroom got up and tried to push his way through the door at once. "I bet the applications got burned up in a fire or something," said a girl nervously. "I've already heard that I got in," said a worried voice. "You don't think there's been some hitch, do you? I mean, they can't take back my acceptance. I've already got my letter and everything."

The halls were teeming with seniors, since practically everyone had applied to State or UNC or both. The humidity meant everybody was having a bad-hair day, and the spirits of the kids around me veered from irritation to giddiness. It had begun to rain, and the slog to the gym was melancholy and full of squeals of complaint as the kids on the edges of the walkway got pushed into puddles.

Once we got to the gym, we moved around aimlessly for several minutes. Quite a few of us parked on the bleachers. Everybody I could see was wearing jeans and sneakers. If campus representatives were in the crowd, they were dressed incognito. I supposed they had been delayed somehow and would be appearing soon. Ten minutes passed and the noise level rose in the gym.

"I've been looking everywhere for you," Penn said, sitting down next to me.

"I'm the quiet type." I smiled at him.

"You realize this is the gremlin again, up to his tricks," he said. Seeing that I was puzzled, he added, "What do you bet this is the same guy who ran off five hundred announcements saying that the Honor Society would be serving free beer after their presentation of *The Importance of Being Earnest?*"

"I didn't hear about that."

"The announcements didn't get sent out, that's why. Mrs. Oliver in the office found them first. No evidence against the gremlin except a smoking Xerox machine."

A harassed, middle-aged woman wearing sensible shoes burst in the side door and seemed momentarily staggered by the size of the crowd. She patted her flyaway hair nervously, cleared her throat, and announced that it was all a mistake, there had been no official announcement. It was all somebody's idea of a joke.

"Told you so," said Penn, standing up.

"I wonder if this stuff is connected to the obscene messages on Casey's computers," I said.

Penn looked thoughtful. "Maybe. We'll find out soon enough, I suppose." He helped me down the bleachers. "Eventually the word will go out about who did it."

"You think so?"

He smiled. "Sure. What's the point of pulling a bunch of crazy stunts if you don't get any credit for it?"

We joined the crowd exiting the gym and drifting back to their first-period classes. I felt safe with Penn's arms around me, and yet I sensed something tentative about his touch, as if he were ready to drop me and run if necessary. He had been hurt, I thought, and I fiercely wanted to promise him that he could depend on me. I was fascinated by the faint glimmer where the hair in front of his ear had been shaved. Farther down was an unexpected flush of color where his razor had scraped the skin. His jaw was solid and his mouth a long, mobile line.

"You remember how much fun it was to play in the mud when you were little?" he asked. "I used to love to feel the mud squishing through my toes."

"Did you ever make mud pies? I was really into mud pies. I tried to bake some one time. It turns out they stink when they're hot."

Penn laughed. "Remember lying on your stomach in the dirt and pushing sticks around?"

"Making forts!" I said promptly. "I used to make caves a lot. I'd pack the dirt on top of my hand and then pull my hand out so there was a hole where it had been. Instant cave."

"Life was simpler then," said Penn wistfully.

We rounded the corner of the administration building and abruptly came upon Bobby Jenkins. His eyes flew to Penn's face, and then he stared at me as if he were seeing me for the first time. I was glad when we had passed him.

"I'd hate to meet him in a dark alley," said Penn.

"He does look kind of scary, doesn't he? But he must have a side we don't see. Don't you think? Otherwise, why would Laurie have liked him?"

"Beats me. I've given up trying to figure out why girls are attracted to guys. It's a mystery as far as I can make out."

I punched his arm. "As if you have anything to worry about."

"Right. Ask anybody." He grinned. "It's been bad for my character, this effect I have on girls, the way they fall at my feet and drool all over me."

His lips were soft and warm on my cheek, and his breath tickled. Then he turned my head and pressed his mouth, warm and damp, against mine. Rain splashed in puddles—*pock, pock, pock*—in a nervous rhythm and the windows of the building rattled with a sudden blast of thunder.

Fourteen

Dear Diary,

I wish the weekend had lasted longer. Now that we're back reality's hitting me with a jolt. I'm doing homework again, listening to the droning of the teachers' voices. Everyone's spirits seem to be sapped. Maybe it's the rain.

I keep thinking of Penn, driving insanely fast, as if he needs to escape. What's going on in his mind when his face goes blank? I've got to stop this—I'm getting morbid. I think we all need to get away again.

The rain continued on and off for days. The front was stalled, I learned when I tuned in to the six o'clock news to check out the weather map. Cheerfully the weatherman assured us no break was in sight. When I ran errands at the grocery store, the dry cleaners, even at the convenience store where I stocked up on chewing gum, the rain was the constant topic of conversation. Store clerks were mournful and claimed to have forgotten what the sun looked like. Farmers who had been praying for rain began to grumble about the crops rotting in the fields. The grocery put up a special display—bags of mildewcide—and although at first I saw an abundance of umbrellas around town, after the first week, when the drizzle continued, people seemed to give up. I saw quite a few walking to their cars bareheaded, letting rain run down inside their collars.

At school, the floors of the hallways were muddy, and damp umbrellas stood in the corners of the school office. Even Nikki had lost the battle to look crisp and neat. Her clothes drooped and her hair fell limply around her ears. Only the gold studs in her earlobes still twinkled bravely. She hadn't had much to say to me since I'd started hanging out with Penn's group, but she did say hi when we ran into each other.

Rain did not, of course, pour constantly. Instead, there was a general dampness, as if we were living in the hollow of a wet sponge.

I ate lunch with Penn and the others every day in the cafeteria, amid the clatter of trays, the zoo noises, and the smell of overcooked spaghetti. But our table seemed set apart from the chaos around us. Even the smells at our table were different. Tessa's bag from home sometimes produced ripe golden apples, crusty bread, and white, sharp-smelling goat cheese that was like a whiff of an herb-covered hillside in the country.

Casey was moody, endlessly preoccupied with the threat of a Valentine's Day computer virus, but even he managed the occasional reluctant smile for Tessa. Her easy affection, like Stephen's sweet smile, became a part of my life. Stephen's pen made starburst blots of black ink on napkins as he sketched physics problems for me. Salt and pepper packets and kernels of corn were lined up at odd intervals in illustration of physical principles. "I think you can grasp it intuitively," Penn would begin hopefully, "if you'd only—" But I would look into his gold-flecked eyes and lose my train of thought.

Afternoons Penn and I spent parked in the Corvette kissing and talking softly. I began to feel a secret thrill of pleasure when I heard people complaining about the weather, because for me the fogged windows of the cars and the soft sounds of the drifting rain had taken on sensuous overtones.

I was amazed at how seamlessly I slipped into

a routine. Stephen and Tessa spoke to me in confidential tones, as if they had known me for years. I think in an odd way they actually welcomed having someone new around to talk to. Though I thought of myself as a private person, it's funny to realize that they must have seen me as quite obvious, as if I were a character who had stepped out of a television show. They were intrigued by my dangly earrings, which were usually in a vaguely hippie style, lumps of jade or garnet with old coins or Hindu symbols swinging from small gold beads. And they were fascinated by my keeping a diary. More than once I had caught Casey staring at its open pages, trying to decipher it.

They were all interested in my habit of leaving behind red M & M's, the crust of pie, the whipped cream of hot chocolate, the nuts out of candy bars. "Don't you ever eat all of anything?" Stephen inquired, eyeing my plate. "Is this part of your religion or because of a childhood trauma or what?"

"I don't like all of it," I replied lamely. "I eat the part I like."

I suppose they were all so used to each other that they had become, in some ways, too close. I seemed new and free. For my part, I grew comfortable around them. I even came to like the smoky smell that invariably clung to Stephen's clothes.

I saw so much of them that I don't see how I could have missed the dark tinge that marked that time. Of course, I noticed things. I was so completely focused on them and spent so much time with them that I was bound to. But they were such little things. Mostly small failures of nerve, I realize now, looking back. Like Tessa's sudden attack of nausea when a waiter brought her steamed shrimp by mistake.

"No! That's not mine!" she exclaimed. She had turned so white she was almost green. "I— I'm giving up shellfish. It's got iodine in it."

This sudden squeamishness seemed peculiar to me, since it was a joke among us that Tessa would try anything—not only sushi, squid, and litchi nuts, but really offbeat things, like chocolate-covered ants. "Taste it first and then I'll tell you what it is" was a line we had all heard from her. But again, it was a small thing.

Several times I had the experience of coming up on the others and being conscious that they had stopped talking abruptly. After the pause caused by my unexpected appearance, they would begin talking again, almost frantically, about something quite innocuous like homework or the theme for the upcoming school dance.

It struck me as strange, because none of them had the slightest interest in school dances. It wasn't that I didn't notice these little inconsistencies. It was more that I refused to let them have any significance. It was too important to me to maintain the illusion that I was completely accepted as a member of the group. I needed to feel that we shared everything.

There were other incidents. I remember once at the cabin hearing muffled voices outside the bedroom door. I glanced over at the other bed and saw that Tessa was up, but she hadn't waked me. Then I heard the distinctive timbre of Penn's voice, though I couldn't make out the words. There was something furtive about the hurried conference, and I had the temptation to tiptoe out of bed and press my ear to the closed door. I swung my legs over the side of the bed, but I was sleepy and I bumped against the lamp. It rocked dangerously and the voices suddenly went silent. I rethought getting up and crawled back into my warm bed. The incident was so unimportant that I went directly to sleep and didn't think of it again. But later in the day, I said casually to Penn, "What were you guys doing up so early? Why didn't you wake me?"

"I thought I heard a raccoon," he said quickly, "so I got up to check on it."

When Tessa came in, I said, "Did you see the raccoon?" She looked puzzled.

"The raccoon we thought we heard this

morning," said Penn, and the warning tone in his voice was unmistakable.

"I don't think it was a raccoon at all," said Tessa at once. "Mysterious noises, that's all. Probably ghosts." But as soon as the words were out of her mouth, she paled and looked as if she regretted what she had said.

It's easy to see, looking back, that I was being left out of something, but at the time it wasn't something I wanted to see. I was happy and that was enough. Every day seemed full of promise.

Often after school we met at The Bakery. I have so many fragmented memories of that off-beat café that they all sort of blend together. The white smears of powdered sugar that smudged our cheeks and fingertips, heart-shaped cookies filled with jam, clouds of steam from cups of hot chocolate are jumbled in my mind with rain streaming down the windows, blurring the colors of the parking lot outside. I associate The Bakery with a strange feeling in which I was pleasantly conscious of the blood pulsing through my body. Happy moments were slipping through my fingers before I was ready to let them.

"You have to try the Linzer tarts," Penn had told me. "They're an old family recipe George's grandmother brought over from Bavaria."

George, the owner of The Bakery, was a plump man with a graying ponytail. He had been a friend of Penn's mother when they were in college, and sometimes he would come over to our table, his face still shiny with steam from the kitchen. "What's the word from bonnie Beth?" he would inquire in a thin high voice.

"She's great," Penn would answer.

"Tell her I said hello" was George's invariable response. The ritual never changed. Beth was always bonnie and Penn always promised to convey George's greetings.

I particularly remember one Thursday afternoon, when Penn and I were the first to arrive at The Bakery. I had gotten a hot chocolate and a handful of cookies. The lights were on, but they did little to lighten the gloom. Outside, the damp-streaked sides of the seed store and the few cars shiny with rain looked surprisingly pretty—abstract and calm like a pencil drawing. A wet crow flew past the window and landed near a puddle. Its feathers were in damp clumps, and it looked cross as it walked about stiff-legged for a moment and tossed a bit of grit with its black beak.

"I wish we could go to the cabin," I said suddenly.

"I thought we might go this weekend," Penn said, "but there's no sign of the weather letting up. Look at it out there."

"Does that matter?" I asked. "We could still

build a fire. We could still play cards." My father had announced he was going to have to attend an out-of-town business meeting over the weekend, and I dreaded being in the house alone.

Penn met my eyes. "Why not?" he said suddenly. "Let's ask the others."

Tessa and Stephen burst in the door, slipped off their jackets, and shook rain out of them. "Get me a peppermint tea, will you, Stephen?" Tessa asked.

She came over to our table and perched anxiously on the edge of her chair. Soon Stephen arrived with a tray carrying two cups of steaming tea and a couple of heart-shaped cookies dusted with powdered sugar.

"They say the river is rising." Tessa looked anxious. "The thing is, it takes days for the water to drain off the surrounding countryside and into the river, but when it does, there could be flooding. It could—it could overflow in the next couple of days."

Stephen sipped his tea. Penn watched him, slightly puzzled. Finally Stephen went on. "They're telling everybody to stay away from the river. Of course, they always do. And—and you know what that means. All kinds of nuts will be out there with canoes trying to shoot the falls. Next thing you know, p-police will be all over rescuing people, bringing out bloodhounds, even."

Tessa shot Stephen an uneasy glance.

"I don't see why people can't show a little sense," Stephen spat out viciously.

I looked first at one and then the other, trying to figure out why they were so upset. "Can't we all stay away from the river? I mean, it doesn't have anything to do with us, does it?" I asked.

Tessa laughed, but the strangeness of the sound made me look at her quickly. She flushed and looked down suddenly at her hands, conscious of my curiosity. "I'll have to tie up my brother, Pete," she said. "He's always into trouble if there's any trouble for miles around. We'll have to put him under house arrest."

I thought I could see why Tessa was on edge. She felt responsible for her younger brothers and sisters, but there wasn't much she could do to control them. Pete was twelve or thirteen. It wasn't as if she could put him in a playpen.

"That's tough," I said sympathetically.

Penn stirred his tea. "Joanna thinks it might be fun to go out to the cabin this weekend. What do you think?"

"I—I guess that's fine." Tessa glanced at Stephen again. "I mean, so far as I know, we're free. We'll let you know if something comes up. Well, look, I'll give you a call tonight when I know more definitely."

I was puzzled. Cords stood out on Tessa's

neck, and her movements were jerky. "Is everything okay?" I asked.

"Fine," Stephen answered. "But if this rain doesn't let up, people are going to start to snap. Doesn't it drive you crazy?"

I blushed. "Actually, I kind of like it."

"Talk about perverted tastes," said Tessa. Pink spots stood out on her pale cheeks.

"Where's Casey?" I asked. My face was getting hot thinking of how much time I spent making out with Penn on rainy days, and I was eager to change the subject.

"He's not coming. He got some new antivirus program in the mail yesterday. He'd be awful company if he were here," said Tessa. "He's developing into a full-blown paranoid."

"Any more gremlin episodes?" asked Penn.

"Casey is convinced a nationwide virus is the school gremlin's work," said Tessa. "That's what I meant about getting completely paranoid. Why would our school gremlin want to screw up NASA's computers? It's absurd."

That afternoon, I had to go out to the drugstore to get shampoo. I was surprised to run into Stephen at the checkout counter. He was paying for three pairs of rubber gloves. When he saw me his color changed. "I'm refinishing furniture," he said abruptly.

I was reminded so forcefully of my mother

and her job refinishing furniture that it was like being hit by a bucket of freezing-cold water. I stared at him, unable to speak.

"They're for putting on the stripper," he explained, his dark eyes watching me. "You have to use gloves when you put it on. They tell you to do that in the directions."

"Sure." I swallowed hard. "I know that."

It seemed as if time were moving in slow motion as Stephen pushed the bills and coins across the counter to the clerk. The moment lasted too long, stretched out like a rubber band pulled almost to its breaking point. I could not seem to make myself blink, and I stared at Stephen's trembling hands, feeling as if my blood had congealed. I wasn't sure I could speak or walk. That's funny, I thought, puzzled. His hands are trembling as if he were guilty, while it's really me who should feel guilty. I'm the one who abandoned my sick mother. It seemed like a peculiar sort of ESP, like the time when Penn called and my heart went thump, but it was the clock that fell off the wall.

The clerk shook open a bag and picked up a pair of the gloves. The flabby rubber fingers looked like bizarre versions of human hands as they disappeared into the crackling paper bag. I had the eerie sensation that they were waving at me, signaling me that they were drowning. I shifted my gaze away from them, shaken, and my eyes met Stephen's. He bit his lip and abruptly shoved his hands in his pockets.

"Not too many people buy three pairs of rubber gloves at one time," said the clerk cheerfully. His blond hair was thin and he wore rimless glasses. "I can't think I've ever seen anybody do that before."

Neither Stephen nor I responded.

"Well, have a nice evening," the clerk finally said.

Stephen clutched the paper bag. "I guess I'd better be getting home," he said faintly. Shooting an alarmed glance in my direction, he bolted out of the store.

I stared after him, watching the glass door swing shut with a faint whoosh. The magazine racks by the counter fluttered.

When I placed my bottle of shampoo up on the counter, my brow was creased in puzzlement. I knew why I had been so thrown by the sight of the rubber gloves. What I couldn't account for was Stephen's seeming even more shaken than I was. The incident could have been captioned like those line drawings in the Sunday comics— What's Wrong with This Picture?

Fifteen

❦

. . . *I guess it's a good thing to be sensitive to things like weather—it means you notice things, you're not walking around asleep, right? Still, it seems weird that Tessa and Stephen are so concerned about the river rising, when they don't seem to care much at all that Laurie is missing. And what does it matter to them if someone's playing practical jokes on Casey?*

They both seem so fragile these days. The way Stephen acted at the drugstore, you'd have thought I'd caught him buying something lethal, not rubber gloves! I don't know when it's okay to talk to them. Sometimes I feel like not much has changed since our first meeting—I'm still an outsider who doesn't know the rules.

*   *   *

A little while after I got in, my father's secretary called to say he would be working late. It seemed to me that he was home less and less. I could not stop myself from going into his bedroom and pulling open a dresser drawer. His underwear stack was thin and the stack of handkerchiefs even thinner. I wondered if he was gradually taking out a few clothes at a time in his briefcase. Perhaps someday I would come home to find out he had moved out of the house completely. What would I do then? Who would pay the bills? My backbone went rigid with fear. I closed the drawers one by one, then balled up a piece of my shirt in one hand and polished around the drawer pulls to erase my fingerprints.

Forcing myself to breathe evenly, I went into the living room. Blood was singing in my ears and I thought I might pass out. I sank down into the vast leather couch and put my head between my knees. This is ridiculous, I told myself. I knew there was no reason for this sudden weakness except an overwhelming lack of confidence in my ability to get along without help.

I retrieved my diary from under the couch, where I had tucked it. The pen was still wedged between the pages. I began writing and, as I had thought it would, the writing calmed me. The sight of the neat coded words—my private language—was a comfort. Between the pages of my diary, at least, I was in control.

I turned back to the first page and stared at it. "This belongs to Joanna Rigsby." My life. It belonged to me. Not my mother. Not my father.

Then I began to write.

> . . . I wonder why I have failed to engage my father's attention. Other people like me well enough. In my blackest moments I sometimes think that I remind him too much of himself and of his own shortcomings. But how can that be? I am not like him. The truth is that I am not like either of my parents. If my father deserts me, I won't fall apart as my mother did. I will manage somehow. I am stronger than my mother—I have to believe that.
>
> I guess I can understand how the divorce tore her apart, though. I tell myself I could live without my father, but could I live without Penn?

A sudden banging on the front door made me jump violently. I sat trembling while the door shook. I leapt up and ran to the peephole, standing on tiptoe to peer out it. The image in the lens was so bizarrely rounded, I might have been persuaded Humpty Dumpty was pounding on my door except that there was something mysteriously familiar about the distorted figure. A ballooning nose came close to the peephole, bizarrely magnified, and the door shook again from angry knocking. I flung the door open, more to quiet the noise than anything, and found myself face-to-face with Bobby Jenkins. He had raised his fist to knock again, and with his wild eyes and his messy hair he looked so frightening, I involuntarily took a step backward.

"Have you seen Blue?" he asked in an anguished voice.

"Blue?" I repeated stupidly. I wondered momentarily if he had gone out of his mind.

"My dog, Blue. Has he come over here?"

"The Irish setter?" I asked.

"A board's out of the fence and he's gone."

"He hasn't been over here." Now that I knew what the problem was, I couldn't help sympathizing. "I'll help you look," I said impulsively. "We can split up and go in different directions. How long has he been gone?"

"It can't be that long. I just fed him a half hour ago."

I reached for my keys on the nearby table and locked the door behind me. "Do you have a picture of him? Lots of people won't be too sure what an Irish setter looks like. It would help."

"Wait a minute." He ran into his house and came out holding two snapshots. "Don't lose it," he said, handing one to me. "These are the only ones I've got."

"We'll have to be sure to ask any golfers we see," I said. "They're outside more than anyone else."

Bobby nodded. His eyes were worried. Muddy water ran in the gutters of the street, and nearby the storm sewer roared as the overflow from the golf course's pond rushed through the big underground pipe. The sky was gray, but no rain was falling. A colorless band rimmed the horizon, as if not clouds but smoke from a distant fire covered the sky.

It didn't take Bobby and me long to fan out through the immediate neighborhood. We sloshed into people's backyards over squishy grass and even knocked on a few doors. A number of backyards were fenced, so that simplified things. Blue was unlikely to have jumped to get into a fenced yard.

At the entrance of the subdivision, as Bobby and I were about to split up and go in different directions, I spotted Blue. He was crouched on the lawn of the country club across the street, hiding his nose between his paws, as if he hoped in this way to avoid our notice.

"Blue!" I screamed. Bobby and I ran over to him. He wagged his auburn flag of a tail and regarded us anxiously. He might not have been a great intellect in the dog world, but he knew he had misbehaved. Bobby grabbed his collar and hooked a leash to it.

"You scared us, you bad dog," I scolded. He was leaping around now, suddenly very frisky.

"Blue!" Bobby bellowed. "You bad, bad dog!" Blue cowered submissively, regarding his master through rolling eyes. "I'd about given up on you, you good-for-nothing dog!" Bobby swore at him.

I took the photo out of my pocket to give to Bobby and looked at it closely for the first time. In it, Blue was sitting next to a fragile-looking girl who was squinting into the sun. I knew I had seen her before. It was Laurie Jenkins, looking the same as she had looked in the slide taken at the sophomore car wash. She was a slightly built girl, with wispy light brown hair, large dark eyes, and a heart-shaped face.

Bobby got a firm grip on Blue and crossed the street at a trot. By almost running, I managed to keep step with him as we headed home. "I was afraid I was never going to see this stupid dog again," Bobby said. "I owe you one." He seemed unaware of how fast he was going. "Laurie named him after the song," he explained. "You know, the one that goes, 'Me and you and a dog named Blue'? It was kind of a joke. I mean, she called him Blue because he was really red."

"Is that Laurie with Blue in the picture?" I panted.

"Yeah."

"Have you heard from her yet?"

"No," he said shortly. Bobby noticed that Blue's tongue was lolling out and slowed down. "Stupid dog," he muttered under his breath.

At last we were standing in front of my house. Bobby's face was dark. "I think Laurie's mad at me," he said abruptly. He turned on his heel, jerked Blue's collar, and then strode back to his house. I watched as the front door closed behind them.

Nobody seemed to want to talk about Laurie, I reflected, and it was hard to think of her as a real person. In photographs her face was abstract, simply an arrangement of light and shadow. She seemed more like someone I had read about than a human being.

I heard my father come in at nine and I made a point of going in to say hello. I had decided it was ridiculous for us to live in the house together as if we were strangers. He measured decaf into the coffee maker, and soon the smell of coffee was in the air. I told him about helping Bobby find his dog. I think I had some dim idea that this was the sort of "sharing" that might be the beginning of a relationship, but he was merely polite.

"Maybe you ought to get a dog," he said. He took a cup out of the cabinet. "Go ahead, if you want. It'd be company for you."

There was an uncomfortable pause while I asked myself if that was his way of saying that I certainly shouldn't count on him for company.

"No," I said. "It wouldn't make sense. Next year I'll be going away to college."

He brightened.

I went back to my room feeling more angry than I could have believed. I entertained myself for some moments with revenge fantasies. I would become famous, and when interviewers asked about my parents I would claim to be an orphan. Or I would become rich and drive my father's company out of business. I would find out his girlfriend's phone number and tell her that he had a secret wife and five small children. Instead, I called Penn.

"Are you okay?" he asked.

"I'm fine."

"You don't sound fine. You sound kind of shaky. Is something wrong?"

"I miss you."

He laughed. "I miss you, too."

After ten minutes of small talk, we uttered

sleepy good-byes. I hung up the phone and went
to bed fully clothed and with the lights on.

The two images I had seen of Laurie Jenkins,
the slide and the photograph, were floating in my
dreams. Then the photograph turned upside
down and joined itself to the top of the slide.
Blue and Tessa had disappeared from the photos
somehow and all that remained was the double
image of Laurie, one from the slide, one from the
photograph, glued together like the twin images
on a playing card. She was the Queen of Hearts,
I thought. Bobby's stormy face appeared like the
Cheshire cat and then disappeared as quickly.
No, that was not quite right, I thought, as the
dream thinned and I became vaguely conscious.
Laurie was not the Queen of Hearts. She was the
Queen of Secrets.

When I got up, my mouth was cottony and
my hair looked as if I planned a career playing
drums for a heavy-metal band. I stared in the
mirror at my disheveled appearance and remembered my disturbing dream. It felt vivid,
as if it had just happened. I hoped a shower
would dispel my feeling that something was
wrong. I stepped out of my clothes and into a
stream of hot water. I could hear the water
gurgling in the pipes as steam billowed in
clouds around me and my body; pummeled by
the spray, I grew pleasantly numb. By the time

I turned off the shower and wrapped a towel around my wet hair, I felt much better.

Yet my dream had cast a spell on me. The extreme neatness of my father's house seemed impossible, like one of those paintings where beds float through blue skies and hats and mustaches exist in complete isolation. An eerie and unsettling coolness had come over me.

I was glad to get to school. I met Stephen near my homeroom. "They're expecting the river to flood tomorrow or the n-next day," he said, running his fingers through his dark hair. "It could be four, five feet above the banks." He passed a palm over his forehead. "I already heard a couple of nuts talk about taking a canoe out."

"Where's Tessa?" I had hardly ever seen them apart, and instinctively I looked around for her.

"Oh, she's here somewhere." I saw that his middle finger was stained yellow from nicotine, and he smelled as if he had been hung in a chimney. "I feel sick," he said.

"Did you eat breakfast?" I asked. I suspected he had had a cigarette instead.

"Maybe not." He glanced around wildly. "What does it matter? Jeez, this weather is driving me bonkers."

The bell rang and crowds surged through the halls. Anxiety crept up my spine like a small and deadly snake. It was not Stephen I wanted to see, with his morbid sensitivity to the weather, but Penn. Penn would calm me down, I thought. But there was no way of getting word to him. I even thought of taping a note to his locker. I felt that desperate. What would I say when he found me? "Hold me," I suppose. "Tell me nothing is wrong."

I couldn't know it at the time, but Penn was more desperate than I. However, I am sure that if I had run into him he would have given me all the false assurance he was capable of. He would have told me that nothing was wrong, even though that was a lie. He didn't like me to be unhappy, for one thing, and for another, his need to present a pleasant surface was strong. But I did not run into him, and there was no hope of seeing him until lunch.

I stayed a few minutes after class to ask Mr. Dockerty a question about the physics homework. Even with Stephen and Tessa's coaching, I was struggling. I was vaguely conscious of more noise outside the classroom than usual, but it barely registered. Dockerty, of course, had long ago tuned out anything that wasn't directly related to physics. He had the intense, small eyes of a fanatic. "How many equilibrium positions does the spring have?" he snarled.

My heart failed me. "A lot?" I whispered.

He slammed his book down on the desk. "An

infinite number," he bellowed.

When I came out of the classroom at last, I was a bit confused and didn't know what to make of the boy directly ahead of me who had his arm around another boy's neck in a hammer-lock grip. My first reaction was that they were fooling around. Another boy staggered against me, almost knocking me down. "Excuse me," I muttered stupidly. Then I spotted Bobby Jenkins, his face distorted in rage, looming directly ahead of me, and I blinked, terrified. I sidestepped just in time as he charged.

A voice shouted, "Fight!" and belatedly I realized I was in the middle of a full-blown melee. I froze like a deer caught in headlights. I am sure none of them intended to hit me, but they were too busy defending themselves from flying punches to worry about whether they ran into me or not. I glanced at the door to the class-room, wishing I could dart in there and cling to Mr. Dockerty, but a muscular guy stripped to his undershirt viciously kicked another boy who was sagging against the door. Before I could turn and run, I saw that Bobby had lifted a kicking boy over his head. While I watched, horrified, he pitched him over the railing.

"My God," someone screamed shrilly. "Bobby's killed him."

Hysterical whoops rose over the cries and hubbub. I bolted for the safety of the surrounding crowd. "Call 9-1-1!" someone screamed. "Don't move him! Don't *move* him!"

"Neil! Neil!"

"He's paralyzed."

As I squeezed my way past the gathered crowd that was surging toward the railing for a better look, I got a chilling glimpse of the lifeless body, spread-eagled and faceup on the grass. The gray sky had drained everything of color, even the blue and red jackets of the boys who were running to the side of the stricken figure.

Could he really be dead? I wondered, hanging over the railing. Next to me a girl, her face puffy and streaked with tears, her nose running unheeded, sobbed. "He's dead," she shrieked. "He's dead!"

But then the figure on the grass moved. A noise scarcely human went up from the crowd. Boys in jackets gathered in an anxious clutch around Bobby's victim as he attempted to prop himself up on his elbows, shaking his head groggily. An angular man in gray pants and jacket was striding toward him, pant cuffs flapping loosely behind his legs, his thin body leaning into the wind.

I felt sick to my stomach and I only wanted to

get away. Staggering to the girls' room, I splashed cold water on my face. What next? I wondered desperately.

On my way to my next class—the halls were almost empty and I made good time. I passed a bunch of lockers at the front of Haggerty Wing, and my eye was caught by a splash of green. A large cardboard leprechaun, green cap, buckled green shoes, and shamrock-print shirt had been taped to one of the lockers. The cardboard figure had been bent into soft waves by the humidity, and a line of perforations made fuzzy half dots along the soles of the leprechaun's shoes. I think I still hadn't pulled myself together after the frightening experience of getting caught in the fight, because I looked at it for a while in puzzlement, thinking that St. Patrick's Day was over a month away. Then I noticed something written on his green cap in Magic Marker. I drew closer. "Casey," it said in round letters. "Catch me if you can!"

Sixteen

Dear Diary,

I need to get away. School is getting to me, and I don't mean just physics. There's definitely something psycho about Bobby Jenkins. I've never encountered anyone so violent. The way he threw that boy Neil over the railing! My flesh creeps every time I think of his limp body lying on the grass. Bobby could have killed him.

I can't wait to get back to the cabin . . .

I could see the river out the window of Penn's cabin. It had risen in its bed, rushing over the roots of trees that reached skeleton fingers to the sky. In the gray light, the water looked angry and dangerous.

Penn sat at the table, his chin cupped in his

palm. I recognized signs of fatigue, the involuntary jerk of a single eyelid, the slow careful movements.

I brushed my hand softly over his hair. "Are you okay?" I asked.

He smiled wanly. "Just need to catch up on my sleep."

Casey was bent over a stack of papers he had collected from the school office—derisive letters sent to teachers on the computer, phony announcements caught before they had been posted. He hoped to find some kind of clue to who was behind the tricks.

"It's like some enemy is after me," he cried, "but that doesn't make sense. I don't have any enemies."

He couldn't let go of the subject. He talked about it obsessively.

"Come on, Casey. It's all been pretty harmless stuff so far," said Penn wearily.

"Harmless?" shrieked Casey, his eyes bulging. "What if they fire me from my job at school? What if they say, 'Casey, old man, if you can't keep control of the computers, we'll find somebody who can.'"

"There's no way they can replace you for the money they're paying you," said Penn.

This thought seemed to comfort Casey. "It's not only the computers," he grumbled. "That stupid elf pasted up on my locker made me a laughingstock."

I wished I had had the presence of mind to strip the cardboard leprechaun off his locker when I saw it.

Penn lifted his eyebrows. "Look at it as an honor that somebody cares enough about you to try to get to you."

"Thanks a lot, Penn. That's a big help," Casey said. He gulped his cranberry juice, and a thin pink dribble ran down his chin. He wiped his mouth with the back of his hand. "I wish Stephen and Tessa would show up. Talk about late—this is ridiculous. I'm getting hungry. What are we supposed to eat for lunch?"

"Don't panic," said Penn. "We can always open a can of tuna."

Casey stared at him as if he had suggested eating poison.

"Did Tessa and Stephen say they were going to be late?" I asked. Where the road was low, water lay in thin, colorless sheets on the pavement. The memory of our own near wreck was still fresh in my mind, and I felt uneasy. "I hope they're all right," I added.

"We'll starve to death before they get here," grumbled Casey. "And don't mention tuna fish to me. Tuna fish isn't food." He turned to me suddenly. "Can't you cook?"

"No!" I looked at him in surprise.

"All girls ought to learn to cook."

"You mean, so we can feed you?" I asked gently. "Maybe you're the one who ought to learn to cook."

"Cooking is women's work. I wish Tessa and Stephen would get here." He clipped the papers together with a heavy paper clip. "Tessa and Stephen, Stephen and Tessa—it's like Tweedledee and Tweedledum. Have you noticed that? Everywhere Tessa goes, Stephen is hanging around her neck. If you ask me, Stephen's got a problem."

Penn groaned softly.

"Seriously!" Casey insisted. "It's really unhealthy. Stephen's *got* to go to Princeton. Why is that? Because Tessa wants to go to Princeton. It's sick."

"They're in love," I said. "I think it's sweet."

"Love, huh!" snorted Casey. "Look at what it's got us into."

I glanced at him quickly, wondering what he was talking about.

"Don't start on that, Casey!" said Penn ominously.

I was startled by the tone of Penn's voice, which was positively dangerous. Casey, too, seemed to recognize that Penn was about to explode. After a nervous glance toward me, he changed the subject.

"Somebody told me you got caught in the middle of that fight at school yesterday," he said. "How did that happen?"

"I have no idea," I said. "I stepped out of Dockerty's class and all around me people were getting throttled."

"You can bet Bobby started it," said Casey. "He's always in trouble. Somebody told me he hit a kid with a brick one time in first grade."

"In first grade!" Penn snorted.

"Okay, laugh, but he ought to be put in reform school. Why, he could haul off and sock any one of us at any time! The guy's dangerous. You know, there's such a thing as law and order, and some of us happen to believe in it—even if you don't."

Penn buried his face in his hands and laughed helplessly. Casey's face turned a nasty shade of red.

What is going on? I wondered. I had the disorienting sensation that I had come in on the second act of a play. I had missed something important; if only I knew what it was. What would they have said if I had asked them flat out what was happening? But I didn't ask. It's more my way to watch and try to figure things out. Only, in this case it wasn't possible for me to figure it out. I was missing some important key.

It was a relief when Tessa and Stephen finally burst in the door. "God, this weather!" Stephen cried. He put a couple of grocery bags down on the table. "Doesn't it feel like the start of a disaster movie? I keep expecting the ground to shake and possessed birds to come zooming out of the sky and tear our flesh to shreds." He looked around vacantly, and I was startled to see that he looked really ill. There were shadows under his dark eyes, and when he put the bags down, his hands trembled.

I took a jug of milk out of the paper bag. "Are you okay?" I asked. "You aren't running a fever or anything, are you?"

Tessa seemed almost to have quit breathing. She was watching Stephen with a look of anxious devotion, and for a moment as we waited for him to speak, we were all frozen in place. In the perfect stillness I heard the rattle of wings as a dove rose in flight outside. Stephen didn't answer. I'm not sure he even heard me. I walked over to the kitchen and put the milk in the refrigerator. Like manikins coming to life, all at once the others moved and spoke.

"Sit down, sweetheart," Tessa ordered. "Just lie down on the couch. We'll put everything away."

Stephen's eyes met hers, and then, as if in response to some secret communication, he meekly collapsed on the sofa.

"You aren't going to throw up, are you?" demanded Casey.

"Don't talk about it," Tessa said. "You know how talking about it always makes people feel sick. I'm starting to feel queasy myself."

"Okay, but do it outside if you're going to do it," said Casey.

Penn left the room and came back with a damp washcloth and handed it to Stephen, who was stretched out on the sofa. "Talk about something, you guys," Stephen said, placing the folded washcloth on his forehead. "I feel awful. Say something to get my mind off it."

"Green, nauseous, disgusting, creepy things!" cried Casey. "Slugs! Slime!"

Tessa took a threatening step toward Casey. She was really angry, but Penn moved in front of him and blocked her way. "I'll shake him until his teeth rattle," Tessa swore.

Stephen smiled. "That's my girl."

"Take a little hint, Casey," said Penn wearily. "If you want to eat, don't make the cook mad."

"Jeez," said Casey. "Can't anybody around here take a joke?"

Penn and I helped Tessa unpack the groceries. Then Tessa got butter out of the fridge, and soon the smell of sautéing mushrooms filled the air. In short order, she served up a perfect omelet. But Tessa had no appetite. She cut her food into sections and pushed it around on her plate, stealing anxious glances at Stephen. He lay on the couch breathing heavily.

After lunch, to my relief, things began to return to normal. Penn built a fire, then got one of the Winnie-the-Pooh books out of the bookcase and began reading aloud. Tessa threw some colored chips on the fire, and the room was aromatic with a faintly pleasant scent. Whether it was the good food or Penn's reading I wasn't sure, but the atmosphere grew lighter.

"I'll make cookies," Tessa cried when Penn closed the book. She leapt up from her post on the floor beside Stephen.

Cabinets opened and closed in the kitchen. I burrowed down in an easy chair and tried to catch up on my diary.

> . . . *The lovely weekend I've promised myself keeps threatening to turn into an only slightly more civilized version of the brawl in the hallway that I walked into yesterday. I can't explain it. Maybe it's the weather, the low-hanging clouds. An electric charge seems to fill the air . . .*

I didn't know what to make of the tense exchanges between Penn and Casey. What did they care whether Stephen wanted to go to

Princeton? What had caused Penn's helpless laughter when Casey launched on a law-and-order speech? I figured I could make sense out of all this later. But for now it didn't matter. The bad moments were over and peace was once more drifting through the cabin. I heard the sharp crack of a breaking egg and Tessa's wooden spoon against the crockery bowl, and looked up to see a cloud of flour rising over the counter. Casey laid a game of solitaire out on the low table in front of the couch.

Penn sat at my feet, strumming his guitar and singing.

When Tessa brought the cookies and hot chocolate, Casey swept the cards off the table. "I was losing anyway," he said.

"Do what I do," suggested Stephen, lifting the washcloth off one eye to peer at Casey. "Cheat."

Penn walked two fingers from my ankle to my knee and, craning his neck, smiled up at me. Melted chocolate was shiny at the corner of his mouth and a few crumbs clung to his bottom lip.

Later on that afternoon, Penn and I managed to slip off for a walk by ourselves. "I hope they don't kill each other while we're gone," he said. "That gremlin at school is about to drive Casey over the edge."

"How did you and Casey ever get to be friends?" I asked.

He looked at me blankly a moment and held a branch aside so that I could pass. As soon as I had gone on, he let the wet branch snap back and a shower of drops hit us both. "No, really," I pressed my question. "You have to admit Casey is hard to get along with."

"You think so? Well, I guess we're all hard to get along with in some way or another."

"Don't you even see what I'm talking about, Penn?"

"I guess I do. Casey can be a little . . . annoying." He smiled. "But we're used to him. We've known each other forever. I don't know. I guess it *is* a little different now. Casey used to be more fun. It seems like this year everything's kind of strange. With everybody waiting to hear about colleges and scholarships." He shrugged.

"Well, you're waiting to hear, too," I said. "And you aren't jumping at everybody."

"It doesn't matter with me," he said. "I don't much care where I go, and my father can pay wherever it is. Besides—" We stepped carefully over a once shallow stream that was now rushing and full. A couple of stones that had been placed at intervals let us get over with only slightly wet shoes.

"Besides what?" I asked.

"You've got a one-track mind. Do you know that?" His eyes crinkled into amused triangles.

"Besides, I have stronger nerves than the others." He looked away. "And a stronger stomach."

"You're just a nicer person."

"You're biased in my favor." He kissed me lightly on the lips.

We sat down on a damp log and idly stripped a few leaves and twigs off a nearby bush. Penn threaded a twig through a leaf, stuck it into a soft chunk of rotting wood, and cleared a place for it. "Ship and sail." He grinned at me.

I peered closely at it. "I think I see the Owl and the Pussycat."

Penn laughed. "That's right. They were in a beautiful pea-green boat, weren't they?"

I clutched a twig with pine needles in one hand while I built a small mound of dirt with the other. Then I crowned the small hill with the twig of pine needles. "Island with hula dancer," I announced proudly.

"Hula dancer?"

I wiggled my twig. *"Aloha!"*

We made rivers, hills, and caves in our little dirt world, and under a log we even found some roly-poly bugs that stayed for a few seconds in a small dirt corral.

We rinsed our hands in the brook, then took handfuls of water back to make a little puddle in our small world. "This makes me feel eight years old again," said Penn, glancing down at the dirt village.

I was looking at him and I smiled. "Not me. I feel pretty grown-up."

His eyes met mine, then he bent his head and kissed me until I lost my breath. We sank down onto the wet forest bed and he kissed my neck and fumbled with the buttons of my shirt.

"I hope this isn't poison ivy." I gulped.

"Wrong kind of leaves," he assured me. "Poison ivy is grooved on one side and smooth on the other." He smiled and then kissed the soft hollow at the base of my neck.

I was losing my bearings. We were alone in a glowing, softly spinning world where the only sound I heard was the pulse of my heart.

"We'd better stop," I said.

"Mmm."

"I mean seriously." I wasn't sure what suddenly made me afraid. Maybe the secrets and the small uneasiness that I had been pushing away came flooding back and made me cautious.

"You know, sometime we could come out to the cabin, just the two of us, if we wanted." He raised his eyebrows.

I bit my lip.

"Or not," he added quickly. "That's okay, too."

I shook my head. Irrational fear flamed up in me, and suddenly I was aware of dark places in my mind that I didn't acknowledge even to myself. There was a lot I didn't know about Penn.

He seemed to read the fear in my face, and his eyes grew dark. "I wouldn't hurt you," he said softly. "I never would." He looked away from me suddenly and his voice sounded muffled. "It's okay. Forget it. It was just an idea."

We struggled to our feet, and I was uneasily aware that dead leaves were stuck to me all over. "Turn around," said Penn. "I'll dust you off."

"No, I'd better do it myself." I knew if Penn touched me, we'd end up kissing. "I'm afraid I've gotten pretty messy."

Penn shrugged. "So, we'll tell everybody we fell down." He slipped his fingers into my hair and kissed me. "It's okay," he said softly. His arm was around my waist. "I love you. You don't have to do anything or be any special way to keep me loving you."

"It's different for you," I said, groping for harmless-sounding explanations of what had just happened. "I mean, it's different for boys."

"You were right the first time," he said. "It's different for me. I'm used to being in over my head."

"We'd better get back," I said. Even though Penn was carefully behaving as if nothing had happened, I felt uncomfortable. We continued on our walk, discussed the identification of poison ivy and the classification of salamanders, everything except what loomed large in my mind. I had the sinking feeling that maybe I would never again be able to recapture the easy feeling we had together.

When we saw the cabin in the clearing ahead of us, the afternoon light glancing off its big windows and the feather of smoke drifting up from its chimney, my uneasiness fell from me. Already I was forgetting my flash of panic when he had kissed me in the woods. It seemed as distant as my old unhappiness when I had lived with my mother. As we stood together gazing at the sleeping house, everything seemed real and good. Overhead, a cardinal chirped. "We're home," Penn said. He put a warm hand on my shoulder and nuzzled my ear.

When we got back to town Sunday afternoon, I had to go to the library. I was behind schedule on my report on causes of the French Revolution that was coming due in A.P. European History, and I ended up driving back late. Going by the gas station on Sunset Avenue, I was startled to see flames leaping from a car that was parked halfway under the service-station canopy. The flames in the night cast a strange flickering light on the oil-stained pavement—it was an eerie sight. The gas pumps at the front of the station were only dim shapes in the foreground, dwarfed in significance by the vast ball of flame beyond them. I could barely make out the frame of the car in the midst of the inferno. The fire leapt over the roof, burning silently with a fierce energy.

I wondered if I should call the fire department and looked around, hoping to see that someone else was doing it. No one seemed to be working at the service station. Perhaps they had gone for help. Then, for the first time, I noticed the two figures standing with their backs to me, on the sidewalk.

I backed up my car to get a better look, and at once I recognized Stephen and Tessa. There was no mistaking the sagging, almost melting look of their clothes seen in silhouette against the flames. I rolled down my window and called to them, but they didn't hear me. I parked along the curb and jumped out. "What happened?" I cried, running over to them. "Have you called the fire department yet?"

"Don't worry." Stephen smiled. "They're on the way."

"Makes quite a show, doesn't it?" Tessa asked. "Considered aesthetically, I mean."

"Heck of a big fire," agreed Stephen.

"Are you sure we aren't standing too close?" I stared at the flames. "What if it explodes?

What if the pumps catch fire?"

"They won't," Stephen assured me. "They have safety devices and whatnot." He waved his arm vaguely.

He seemed so calm it crossed my mind that he might be drunk, but when I looked at him sharply, he seemed the same as usual. Only, if anything, more peaceful.

"Whose car is it?" I asked.

"Mine," said Stephen. "The car parked next to it looks like a goner, too."

"Your car? How did it—what happened?"

"I tossed a lighted cigarette down." Stephen shrugged. "The rest is evident."

"They warn you not to smoke or light a match around gas tanks," Tessa pointed out.

"No danger I'll forget after this." I was gazing at the fireball. "I really think we should stand farther away."

"We're plenty far away. Besides, if it were going to explode, I think it would have done it by now, don't you, Stephen?" Tessa glanced at him.

"I think so," he said.

I hesitated, fascinated by the spectacle of the flames, but strongly wishing to put distance between myself and so much flammable gasoline. I backed away, toward my car. "Do you two need a ride home?" I asked.

Tessa smiled. "You're sweet. But I think we'd better wait for the fire department."

When I drove away, they were still standing there, shoulders hunched, their hands thrust in their pockets, their eyes fixed on the flames.

Seventeen

Dear Diary,
How could Tessa and Stephen act so calm? It's almost as if they set the fire on purpose. But why would they do that? They couldn't have done it—could they?

When I told my father about the burning car, his only comment was that warnings against smoking are clearly posted in gas stations. I called Penn to give him a report and he said that he would hate to be in Stephen's shoes and having to break it to his parents. He also doubted that insurance would cover it, since Stephen had been so careless.

The vision of the car in flames had made a strong impression on me. The next day, at school, I still needed to talk about it. I ended up stopping Nikki Warren in the hall. "It was incredible. Flames were shooting out everywhere," I said. "You can't imagine what it was like."

"Cars burn all the time like that in movies," she said.

"Believe me, it's different when it happens right before your eyes."

"Look!" said Nikki, pointing skyward. "The sun has come out."

I suppose it's a comment on how long the drizzle had gone on that the appearance of the sun seemed to be more important than what had happened to Stephen's car. Dark clouds hung over much of the sky, but bright patches of brilliant sky had appeared and the contrast was striking. Sunshine lay in pools on the sidewalks and made the grass glitter. As if a dirty film had been lifted from our sight, colors became brilliant.

When I saw Stephen later, I asked how his parents had taken the news that his car had gone up in smoke. He said pretty well, considering. They were relieved that he hadn't been in the car when it burned.

A florist's van was parking in front of my house when I got home from school. A young man in pastel overalls got out carrying an enormous bouquet of roses. The red blazed fiercely in the sunshine.

"Are you Joanna Rigsby?" he asked.

I nodded and took them from him, my heart pounding. The long-stemmed roses made an unwieldy bouquet and dwarfed me. Through the forest of fat green stems and tightly furled roses, I saw the flash of the delivery man's white teeth. "Hey, he must like you a lot, huh?" he pried.

I was speechless. The delivery man sprang back in the truck and the truck roared away. I was left smiling idiotically as I was engulfed by a cloud of his engine exhaust.

I bore the roses carefully into the house. Not that they looked at all delicate. Their thick stems were well defended with thorns and the roses themselves were fat and deeply red. Their petals were so vivid that I half expected them to move. Once I put the vase on the dining-room table, I took the card out of its small envelope. "My love for you is deep and strong," it said. "Penn." The slanting letters of his script blurred as I stared at the words. A swell of emotion engulfed me, and for an instant I felt as if I were drunk with love. I half expected a bolt of lightning to strike me dead for daring to be so happy.

Valentine's Day! I remembered, with a sudden shock. I wondered if the virus had wrought havoc with Casey's computers.

I wasn't able to reach Penn to thank him until early in the evening. He came to the phone sounding rather out of breath. "I've been slaving at the library on that paper for history," he said. "Do you think a person can go insane from doing research?"

"Penn, I love you," I whispered.

"What?"

"I love you," I repeated.

He sounded pleased. "Oh, the flowers got there."

"Nobody's ever sent me flowers before."

"I love you, too," he said.

"I wonder if the virus wiped out Casey's computer?"

He laughed. "The virus was a no-show. Casey hasn't quit worrying yet, though. Now he's wondering if the computer bandit got his dates off and his computer is going to self-destruct tomorrow. It's going to take him a while to calm down."

"Let's talk some more about how we love each other," I said. "I liked that part."

"From the first minute I saw you," he said, "I knew this was something important. I love the serious way you look. I love the way you smell. I love to hold your hand and feel the blood pulsing through your veins. I love to kiss you."

I sighed happily. "It's wonderful the way you

don't have any trouble expressing yourself."

"Also I love your mind," he added. "I don't even care if you beat me at Scrabble."

The colors of my room seemed to blur and swim before my eyes as I lost myself in a daze of relief and happiness. I would have stayed on the phone forever just for the pleasure of hearing Penn breathe, but I remembered that he had to work on his history paper, so I forced myself to say good-bye.

My father didn't come in until midnight. I was unable to sleep, so pleasantly disturbed was I by the roses. I had tucked the card from the flowers into my bra close to my heart, as if it had magical power to heal my every hurt.

"Good grief!" I heard my father's voice in the living room. Soon his face appeared through the crack in my bedroom door. "Who sent the flowers? The boyfriend?"

I nodded.

"He's probably trying to seduce you," he said. "Watch out."

I took my breath in so sharply, I thought I might choke. Hate for my father and his coarse mind flamed up so quickly in my heart that I was astonished at myself. He must have seen the change in my expression, because he quickly added, "I was only kidding. They're very pretty." But his eyes clouded at once. "A dozen of them. He sent a dozen. Jeez. I wonder—" He closed the bedroom door. I supposed he was wondering if he should have sent Jennifer roses. Knowing my father, if he gave her anything at all, it was probably an up-to-date guide to the tax code.

Tuesday's paper had a brief account of the accident involving Stephen's car. Two fire trucks had responded to the call; Stephen's vehicle was a total loss and the vehicle parked next to it had sustained damage estimated at three thousand dollars. But that story was only a small item on an inside page. The front page was taken up with extensive accounts of flooding over most of the state. A group of campers had been reported missing and search parties had looked five hours in the flooded areas before being notified that the campers had phoned relatives from a nearby motel. Two college students in a rented canoe had capsized in the rushing water near the falls. The surging water had sucked the canoe under and the students had clung to a half-submerged tree for six hours, too far from shore for a rope to be thrown to them, until they were plucked to safety by rescue workers in a helicopter.

The school's electrical system shorted out. All Tuesday the lights flickered and the bells rang at odd times. The clocks on the walls got behind. I began to have the uneasy feeling that my familiar world was coming undone. The predictable order of things—season and weather, electric light switches and clocks—seemed to be losing the glue that held it together.

When I went to my locker Wednesday morning, I was staggered to find Casey and Koo entangled in a hot embrace.

"Excuse me?" I said. "Excuse me? I need to get to my books."

Casey beamed at me. "Hi, Joanna. Do you know Koo?"

"We've met." I nodded at her as I grabbed my books.

"Can you believe this little cutie was our gremlin?" Casey laughed.

My jaw dropped and I stared at Koo. Her sooty eyes met my gaze through a scraggly curtain of hair. Some ratty tendrils had been pulled over her forehead, an effect that was supposed to seem sexy, I suppose. Her pouting lips were bloodred.

"Yes siree," Casey went on. "She had me rattled but good."

Koo laced her fingers behind his neck and gave him a smoldering look. "I'm going to keep you off balance," she said.

The whole thing was so bizarre, it seemed like

a bad joke—Koo nuzzling Casey, her rice-powder white nose pressing against his face. It couldn't be happening. Finding both of them so unattractive, I suppose I was amazed to learn that they were attracted to each other.

As soon as I was able to get my books together, I fled. But even stranger things had happened, I reminded myself. Penn had once gone out with Koo. Penn! It seemed almost impossible to imagine. He was so gentle and civilized. Recalling the odd smell of the incense and body oils Koo put in our locker, for an insane moment I wondered if Koo had somehow cornered the market in pheromones, those aromas that are supposed to have such an electric effect on the courtship practices of cockroaches. If the formula for a workable love potion was actually stashed in the bottom of our locker, then I supposed Koo would get her face splashed all over the cover of *Time* magazine and be Woman of the Year. In my state of mind, anything seemed possible.

When I ran into Tessa outside the cafeteria, I grabbed her. "Casey is hooked up with Koo. Can you believe it? It turns out she was the gremlin all the time. She was the one who pulled all the practical jokes and sent the obscene messages over the computer. And get this—he *likes* her. After practically going nuts about the stupid gremlin for ages, now suddenly he decides he thinks what she did is cute!"

"You have got to be joking!" Tessa was pale. "Are you sure?"

"I swear to you, they were all over each other right in front of my locker. I had to kick them aside to get at my books. And I got it from Casey's own lips that Koo was the gremlin."

"I guess she was trying to get his attention," Tessa said slowly.

"As if she needed help getting anybody's attention!"

"I suppose she was trying to impress him. You know how condescending Casey is about girls. Maybe she wanted to show him she's a force to be reckoned with." Tessa gulped. "I've got to tell Penn and Stephen right away."

Suddenly I felt cold. "You don't think Casey will bring her out to the cabin, do you?" I couldn't bear for my sacred retreat to be polluted by Koo's presence.

"He couldn't, could he?" said Tessa. "Penn would have to invite her. N-no. I'm sure not even Casey would do that."

"He might show up with her out of the blue. That's exactly the sort of thing Casey would do."

"Casey wouldn't do that," Tessa assured me. "He's not going to bring her around where Penn is."

"You mean, he'd be afraid that Penn might— might take her back?" I felt a sick clutch in my stomach at the thought.

Tessa touched my shoulder. "Not that Penn would ever do that, of course. Don't get that idea. Koo was a weird stage Penn went through after his mother left. There was nothing serious between them, really."

I wanted to believe her, but she was speaking in deliberately soothing tones as if to a child. I could hear kindness in her voice, and it frightened me.

"Casey's so insecure, though." Tessa's brow was painfully knit. "You know how he is. Sometimes I just can't tell what he will do. Do you know what I mean?"

I swallowed. "Of course." I was insecure myself. I had been struck by a vision of Casey and Koo making out in front of my locker, but Casey's face melted and became Penn's. Desolation leaked into my heart.

"This is bad," Tessa said.

At lunchtime I saw Casey and Koo together in the back of the cafeteria. I watched as Koo rubbed her finger on a butter pat and then smeared it all over Casey's round nose until it was shiny. Then she sat in his lap and began licking his nose. Half the cafeteria was watching in horrified fascination, and the other half was pretending not to notice. Casey smiled broadly.

Tessa stole a glance at them and groaned softly. "Puts you off your appetite, doesn't it?"

"Jeez!" said Stephen, averting his eyes.

Penn shook his head. "Gross."

Tessa shuddered. "That girl will do or say anything, and Casey's acting like her love slave. Doesn't that bother you?"

The three of them exchanged troubled glances.

"He's just fooling around." Penn glanced at the table at the back of the cafeteria where Koo and Casey sat. "They probably don't even talk to each other."

"What do you bet you're wrong?" said Tessa ominously. "What do you bet Casey can't resist showing off to her and making himself look like some big, important man."

An uneasy silence fell over the table.

Tessa tore her roll in half with a violent movement. "Somebody had better talk to him."

"Come on, Tessa," Penn said. "You know there's no use talking to him."

Stephen began humming "When a Man Loves a Woman." Tessa glared at him. "How can you?" she cried.

Stephen fell silent.

"It'll probably be all right," said Penn, sounding unconvinced. "How long can it last, anyway?"

"Russian roulette doesn't last long either," Tessa said.

I meant to go by my locker after school to drop off some books, but as I approached, I saw a clutch of ratty-haired girls in front of it, their arms around each other, football-huddle style. Since I couldn't see any of their faces, for a second I had the disconcerting impression that Koo had multiplied and was conferring with two of her clones. Then I noticed that one of them had shaved one side of her head and the glistening white of her scalp made a startling contrast to the uncombed black hair on the other side. A moment's reflection told me that Koo, like everyone else, must have friends and no doubt they dressed similarly. When I got closer, I caught some of what they were saying.

"He never guessed it was me messing with the computer and all. He was going crazy trying to figure it out." Could that actually be Koo giggling? I thought, amazed. I couldn't imagine her laughing. Their heads were so close together, it was hard to be sure. "He's real smart, but he's kind of sweet, too," Koo went on. "He wants to go to MIT, this real fancy school up north, but he doesn't know yet if he got in."

"Must be nice to be a brain."

"He's *so* cute, Koo. Weird, but cute," said a high squeaky voice.

"I always did have kinky tastes," said Koo complacently.

"We know all about that," said the girl with the shaved head. "Tell us about—"

I strained to hear the last word. Did she say "him" or "Penn"?

Suddenly I didn't think I could face asking the three of them to move so I could get in my locker. I pivoted and hurried away down the hall. Laughter echoed behind me.

Blindly I stumbled in the direction of the student parking lot. Him—Penn. What was wrong with me? Why couldn't I seem to think straight? Coming around the corner of the building, I ran smack into Bobby Jenkins.

"Whoa!" he said. "Where's the fire?" His thick arms strained at the seams of his shirt as he held me at arm's length. He looked closely at my face. His hair was greasy and uneven stubble alternated with a few odd zits. "You look like you need a stiff drink," he said.

"What are you doing at school?" I said. "I thought you'd been suspended for fighting."

"Ancient history. That was last week. They only threw me out for a couple of days," he said airily. "Now Bobby's back, and I'm celebrating with a TGIF party tomorrow. You come, you hear?"

"I'll see," I hedged, "but I've got an awful lot of work to do."

His face darkened. "I guess you think you're too good to come to my parties. Is that what you're thinking?"

"No!" I protested, alarmed at his expression.

"I notice you always have time to go off with Penn on the weekends. Guess you two are shut up somewhere with piles of homework, huh?" He guffawed. "Tell you what—somebody you know is going to be there. Casey, the so-called genius."

"No, really?" I said weakly.

"That Koo is wild. Can you believe her and Casey, the pie-faced computer geek? I wonder what you'd get if you crossed them? A pie-faced nymphomaniac, I guess."

It was interesting that Bobby disapproved of the match between Casey and Koo as much as Casey's friends did.

"Look." He glared at me. "I want to see you at my party, huh? I'm taking roll." He gave me a playful shove that sent me reeling, and galloped off.

I thought I had an inkling now why the neighbors didn't call the police when Bobby had a party. They were probably scared he would slash their tires. I was actually standing there feeling worried that if I skipped his party he would be mad at me. He reminded me of those pro football players who win fame and fortune mowing down colleagues on the playing field and then later go to jail for running over their wives and creditors with the family Jeep. I could not imagine trying to reason with him.

Penn was leaning against my car, waiting for me when I got there. He frowned. "Why were you talking to Bobby?"

"He wants me to come to his TGIF party."

Penn tilted his head and looked at me with a quizzical smile. His fingers ruffled my hair. "You can't do that. You're going out with me tomorrow night."

"Maybe we'd better make it sort of late," I said, uneasily thinking of Bobby's playful shove and the threat implicit in it. He was not a person I cared to cross. "I really think I ought to look in on Bobby's party. He's going to think I'm a snob if I don't show up."

"What do you care what he thinks?" Penn frowned. "I don't like it, you going over there without me. All those guys'll be drunk."

"Casey's supposed to be there."

"Casey?" Penn sucked in his breath. "Casey's going to Bobby's?"

I grinned. "I'll be able to give you a full report on his misbehaving."

"All right." He didn't smile.

"But don't worry," I promised, "I won't stay long."

*　　*　　*

Dear Diary,

These days I have the constant feeling that I'm missing something. It's as if the others have some secret means of communication. I suppose it's because they've all known each other so long that each knows how the others will react. I wonder if Laurie was that way, too.

I didn't understand what was going on at lunch today. The idea of Casey's showing off to Koo was scary in some vague, hard-to-define way. But why the whiff of panic I sensed rushing over our table? What are they all so afraid of? And how does Laurie's disappearance fit into the picture?

Eighteen

. . . But why? Why is Penn making an issue of my going to the party? He never talked about Bobby's party not being safe. Why does he care whether or not Casey goes? What's the big deal?

Our street began to fill up with cars as soon as it got dark. They were parked helter-skelter, some pulled up onto the grass, sunken black tire tracks marking their paths. A girl holding a glass tumbler in one hand was stepping from the hood of one car to another.

"Aw, come on down, Jess," a boy in the shadows whined.

"I'm not finished," she said. The streetlight glinted on the glass as she moved from one car to another. I could hear the metal buckling under her bare feet and then snapping back when she shifted her weight. I cast an uneasy glance at my own car. It was parked close to the house, not near enough to any other car for Twinkletoes to be interested in it.

The night air was cold, and I pulled my jacket tight around me as I walked across the street to Bobby's house.

Heat and noise hit me in the face when I pushed open the front door. My first impression was confused—close-pressed bodies, the smell of beer and smoke—but after a moment I began to make sense out of the chaos.

"Hello!" Bright eyes peered up at me through a cascade of thin black braids. "Where's Penn?"

Something about the girl before me was faintly familiar. "I'm Reba!" she shouted. "Reba Rogers. I sit next to you in physics class—Rigsby, Rogers, Rundgren, Shippen?" She giggled.

"Oh, yes." The black braids had thrown me off, as had the sassy smile. The Reba Rogers who sat behind me in physics wore her hair in a ponytail and always looked half-asleep.

"I thought you were going out with Penn Parrish," she shouted over the music.

"I am," I shouted back. "This isn't"—I made a helpless gesture—"his kind of thing."

She nodded vigorously. "Well, a girl's got to have some fun, doesn't she?" A Neanderthal type grabbed her from behind, and I briefly wondered if I should try to help her, but she was giggling so I decided it was okay.

"Jo-Jo, baby!" Bobby engulfed me in his elephantine arms and squeezed hard.

"Oomph," I said. Fortunately, he soon let me go. "Where's Blue?" I shouted in his ear.

"In the backyard," Bobby bellowed. "He doesn't like the music. It makes him howl."

The music was okay, I guess, for those who are attracted to industrial noise. I like melody myself.

Now that Bobby had seen me, I figured I didn't have to stay much longer. I made my way through the crush back to the kitchen for a soda. As I flipped open my cola and moved out of the kitchen, a shriek made me turn sharply. I found myself looking directly at Casey, who was about ten feet away from me. I was startled to see he was clutching a pair of slender legs. My eyes rose and I saw that Koo was riding on his shoulders. Her black stockinged feet drummed on his sweatshirt as she reached for the brass chandelier that hung over the table in the dining room. "Back up! Back up!" she shrieked. "I've *got* it." The chandelier began to swing dangerously from its chain. Koo was bouncing with excitement, her talons clutching Casey's red hair. "Go, horsy!" she cried. I could see the underwiring of her black bustier cut-

ting into the powdery white flesh under her arms.
It was hot, and when they turned around I saw
trickles of sweat making wet streaks down her
back, disappearing into the lace edging of the
corset.

"I'm the king!" Casey crowed. "The king of
the hackers." Drawn by sick fascination, I followed them into the living room. Casey had
shown no sign of recognizing me, and judging by
the glazed look in his eyes, he was pretty much
out of it.

I couldn't help wondering what Bobby's
mother thought of his parties. Even if Bobby
cleaned like a demon, I guessed there would be
certain inevitable wear and tear connected with
having wild bashes. Casey clomped around the
living room, and Koo took playful swipes at the
lamps in the room, which rocked precariously. I
deduced that her aim was to get all the lamps
rocking at the same time. But due to the tremen-
dous crush of bodies in the living room, Casey's
progress around the room was slow. The first
rocking lamp subsided before Koo could set the
third one going.

Out of the noise of the party with an eerie
clearness came the thin whine of Casey's voice.
"I've broken into NASA's computer, Berkeley's
computer," he said to no one in particular. "I've
broken into the Dep-Department"—his thick

tongue stumbled over the syllables—"of Motor Vehicles. I'm the king, man!"

The lamp by the bookcase fell over and hit the carpet. There was a shower of sparks. A skinny boy had the presence of mind to pull the plug. He knelt down and rubbed his finger anxiously over the black burn mark on the carpet.

"Lemme down!" Koo was crying. "Lemme down, Casey. I want to change the CD."

Casey knelt, groggily steadying himself against the sofa with one hand. Koo climbed off his shoulders. When she had disappeared into the crowd, I went over to Casey. "Casey," I said, "are you all right?"

His eyes turned toward me but they weren't entirely focused. He was still kneeling, looking a little puzzled but making no effort to stand up.

"Do you want me to get you a cup of black coffee?" I asked.

"I don' drink coffee," he said, looking hurt. "Coffee is bad for you. Where's Koo?"

"She's gone to change a CD. Listen, Casey, do you need a ride home?" The idea of giving Koo and Casey a ride home didn't thrill me, but neither did the notion of finding their bodies spattered all over the pavement the next morning. "Or I could call a cab," I said, having a better thought.

"I'm fine." He frowned at me. "I'm jus' having

a good time. I have a lot of stress in my life. I need to have fun."

"Give me your car keys," I said.

He showed no sign that he had heard what I said, so I reached into his pocket. "That tickles," he said. "What are you doing? You'd better not get fresh with me. Koo won't like it." He smiled and leaned back until he lost his balance, but by then I had the keys in my hand. He sat on the floor, his head lolling against the couch, and smiled at me. "Koo is a real woman," he said. "She's great." He made a sloppy effort at outlining an hourglass shape with his hands, but his coordination wasn't up to it. He looked like a clumsy person trying to practice a martial art. "She's no dummy, either. People think Koo is a dummy, but they're wrong, wrong, wrong!"

"You'd better go to sleep now," I said nervously. I was afraid Koo was bearing in our direction. Someone, at least, was plowing through the crowd headlong. There were signs of confusion, and I heard cries of indignation. I grabbed my jacket. A skinny boy spilled beer on me. "Sorry," he said, flushing scarlet. Ducking past him, I made my escape out the front door.

The cold outdoor air was like a blessing. I breathed deeply until the cold cut my lungs. Then I watched my breath make a cloud in the night air. I felt I had witnessed a disaster. The memory of Casey's slack lips and his lolling head made me queasy. Hugging myself against the cold, I ran down the steps and hurried back to my own house.

When I got inside, I stripped and took a shower. I hated the way the smoky, beery smell of the party had clung to me. I brushed my teeth and gargled, trying to shake the feeling of being tainted. Then I sat on the couch and wrote about Bobby's party in my diary.

> . . . *I keep thinking of hell as it's pictured in paintings from the Middle Ages. It's always crowded in those pictures, the sinners packed cheek to jowl, howling for drink with their tongues hanging out. You might think the painters had been to Bobby's party . . .*

Penn showed up at my front door at ten. "I had to park on Brookner Avenue," he said. "We're going to have to walk a couple of blocks." His hair was damp, as if he had just gotten out of the shower, and there were grooves in it where it had been combed. He put his arms around me, and my eyes half closed in contentment. Colors around me blurred to the look of springtime.

"You're the best thing that's happened to me

in a long time," he said huskily. He squeezed me until I was short of breath, a long embrace as if he didn't want to let me go.

"I love you," I gasped.

He grinned. "Good. We've got a good thing, don't we?"

"The best." I beamed at him.

Penn looked around. "Have you noticed how we never stay at your house or my house? We never do."

"It's not home," I said. I wasn't exactly sure why, but I felt intensely uncomfortable in my father's house and was always glad to get away.

"I know what you mean. I feel funny about my house, too, since my mother left. As if there's some sort of bad feeling radiating from the walls. I don't want to take you there, because I'm afraid the bad vibes might rub off."

"Nothing will make me stop loving you," I said warmly.

"I hope not. But I feel kind of superstitious about it. Like, the house wasn't exactly lucky for my mom and dad."

"We've got the cabin. We've got the 'Vette," I said.

"Yeah, we've got the world." He helped me into my coat. "We don't need this place."

I squeezed his hand.

"Okay, let's go. It's gotten colder," he said regretfully.

We clasped hands and plunged outside.

Despite the chill, I was warm. I felt as if a light bulb had been turned on inside me. Mist hung in the air and the haloed streetlight cast an unearthly glow on the endless parked cars. The neighborhood looked strange in the foggy night, and I had the unnerving feeling we were setting out into some fifth dimension. I clung tightly to Penn's hand as if I were afraid of getting lost.

"Let's go somewhere we can sit under a blow dryer." Penn shivered.

"We could have a picnic in the ladies' room," I said. "They have those hand blowers in there."

"Maybe we'd better settle for donuts and cocoa," Penn suggested. "It ought to be warm enough at Donut King."

I stumbled at the curb and suddenly Penn swept me up in his arms. "Put me down!" I squeaked. "You'll drop me!"

"How could I drop you?" He grinned. "I'm never going to let you go. Now you know the truth—I'm as overbearing as my dad."

"Seriously? Put me down, Penn! What if you trip?"

"I'm not going to trip. But okay."

Laughing, I slid down out of his arms, and he kissed me.

Brookner Avenue was a traffic artery, but it was deserted at this hour. I heard a solid click from a metal box on a post, and the light changed from red to green.

Penn opened the Corvette's door for me. As soon as I sank against the leather seat, the windows began fogging and the traffic light ahead of us took on a smeared haziness.

"I haven't told you about Bobby's party yet," I said. "It was gross."

"Told you so," said Penn, getting in behind the wheel.

"I had to take Casey's car keys away from him. I don't think he even saw what I was doing. I guess I'll mail them back to him—anonymously. I don't want him to be mad at me."

As I began to tell Penn about Casey's behavior, he seemed to be holding his breath. I recognized that peculiar silence that falls when someone is anxious not to miss a word.

"Hey, you may have saved his life," Penn said. I could see the muscles in his cheeks tensing. "Don't worry about it." We passed under the traffic light, and a fireworks of wavy reflections flashed on the car's shiny red hood.

"He was bragging about what a computer genius he was," I said. "Calling himself king of the hackers."

Penn didn't say anything, but I sensed that something was wrong. The warm happiness that had enveloped us only moments before seemed to have vanished. It was as if a chill had fallen over Penn.

"Casey was acting completely insane," I continued, glancing at Penn uneasily. "I hope he's not mad at me about the keys. You do think I did the right thing, don't you? To take them?"

"What?" Penn was puzzled. "Oh, the keys. Yeah, sure, you did the right thing. What else was Casey spouting off about?"

"He said he broke into NASA's computer." I watched Penn's pained reaction. "I kept expecting an FBI agent to jump out from behind the couch and arrest him."

"Anything else?" Penn asked, his voice quiet.

"Well, he was talking all about how he had broken into all kinds of computers and how he was king of the hackers and how Koo was a real woman. He was making a complete fool of himself."

"Was anybody paying any attention, do you think?" Penn peered away from the road for an instant.

"He was so obviously out of it. Really, it's hard

to believe anybody would take him seriously."

The steering wheel slid through Penn's palms, making a whispering sound. When we paused at a traffic light, Penn put his elbows on the steering wheel and rested his head on his arms. The red from the light glowed on his hair.

"Are you okay?" I touched his arm. "Penn? Did I say something wrong?"

His eyes met mine. "Do you mind if we skip the donut shop? I've got a headache." The light changed and the car behind us honked. The Corvette shot ahead.

"Of course I don't mind," I said, alarmed. "Turn around. I'll run in the house and get you some aspirin."

"I have something I can take for it when I get home. My dad gets all these free samples. There are piles of them in the bathroom. I'm sorry about this," he said.

"No, don't worry about it. Are you sure you're okay to drive?"

"I'm fine." Penn's face was a tightly drawn mask of pain, and I had a peculiar and disturbing shock of recognition. It was the same look that drew me to him the day I saw him in the library. The windows of the car were fogged, and I rubbed a little circle clear to look out. But the simple motion made my stomach twist in fear. I suppose I was reminded of the day the Corvette had skidded in the rain. As we turned back onto my street, I wiped my damp palms on my jeans.

"Don't walk me up to the house," I said. "Hurry home and take something for that headache."

"I'll see you tomorrow," he said. When he touched my hand, I was shocked that his fingers were stone cold.

"Good night," I said. I regarded him with anxious eyes. "Get some sleep."

I stood in the street for a couple of minutes watching the Corvette's taillights move down the street. Soon the car was swallowed by the thick fog. I stood there for some minutes watching the traffic go by, paralyzed with anxiety. At last I turned and walked back to my house. Across the street, Bobby's party boomed into an indifferent night.

Nineteen

Dear Diary,

Was it my imagination, or was Penn's headache brought on by the story about Casey?

Maybe I should have listened to him and not gone to the party. Maybe I shouldn't have said anything about Casey. I don't know—none of it makes sense to me anymore. Everything's spinning out of control.

My father was away again. I was vaguely aware of that much. His secretary had called to tell me where he was going, but his excuses had begun to blur one into another. I no longer cared why he didn't come home.

I dialed Penn's number and listened to it ring, six, ten, fifteen times. I had waited till the late

morning to call him, thinking that he might have
slept late. It had never occurred to me that he
wouldn't answer, and at first I couldn't believe it.
I hung up and redialed, thinking maybe I had
gotten the number wrong. I had an impulse to go
over to his house, imagining him lying helpless
on the floor.

It seems odd, but I had never been to Penn's
house and wasn't sure how to find it. I also had a
slight dread of encountering his father, whom I
had never met. Maybe that's why I called Tessa
instead of jumping in my car at once. I had the
vague sense that perhaps she would know where
he was. The voice that answered the phone at
Tessa's house was clear and piping. I could hear
the music of Saturday cartoons in the background. "Tessa's at Penn's cabin," reported the
child. "She won't be back till Sunday."

"Are you sure?" I asked numbly.

"Yeah. She's gone. Pete! Put that down or I'll
kill you!"

"Thank you." I hung up. There was some
mistake, I told myself. As if in a trance, I called
Stephen's house. A pleasant-voiced woman answered. "Stephen is spending a couple of days
with his friend Penn in the country," she said.
"May I tell him who called?"

"No, thanks," I said dully. "It isn't important."

I sat by the phone, my thoughts spinning out

of control. Why had they all gone off this way
without telling me? Had I somehow offended
Penn? Did he really have a headache last night?
Or did he merely want to get away from me? My
world rocked, and the pain I felt was so intense it
found relief only in immediate action. I grabbed
my car keys and ran out the door.

I'm not sure I thought at all as I drove to the
cabin. "No!" I said aloud. Then I caught a glimpse
of myself in the rearview mirror, white and
drained. I touched my chest where I could feel the
card lying stiffly next to my heart. For days I had
been wearing it like a talisman. *My love for you is
deep and strong.* My father's voice rang in my ears:
"He's trying to seduce you." I remembered Nikki
Warren's vague warnings.

"This can't be happening," I said aloud. "It
can't be. Something is wrong."

A car passed mine with a noise like a sigh.
The day was gray and cold, and pines threw their
shadows in bars across the highway. Smoky wisps
of black cloud moved swiftly across the sky, driven
by an unseen wind. HENDERSON'S BAIT AND
TACKLE—2 MILES said a peeling sign. I realized I
was close to the cabin. Now that I was almost
there, it hit me suddenly that I hadn't planned
what I was going to do. What would I say when
they came to the door? My thoughts trailed away
helplessly. Did I really want to hear Penn say out

loud that he didn't want to see me? Perhaps I could act as if I just happened to be passing by. But what errand could conceivably have brought me out deep into the woods where the only point of interest was a bait-and-tackle shop?

The blank space indicating the driveway appeared in the wall of trees. I could park outside and watch the house for a while and not even knock. I wrenched my wheels into a sharp left turn, without having decided.

But as soon as I saw the peaked roof of the cabin I realized that no one was there. Dead leaves blew across the clearing as I let my car roll to a stop. The dirt had been swept clean by the wind, and the only fresh tire tracks in the soft dirt were my own. Puzzled, I got out and climbed the steps. Standing at the front door, I bent to peer in the huge plate-glass window that formed the front wall of the living room. Inside, all was tidy and empty. No groceries were heaped on the counter, no bags of clothes were laid against the back of the couch. The vague untidiness that was a regular feature of our weekends at the cabin was not in evidence. The place might have been closed up for years.

This has to be some sort of mix-up, I thought uneasily. Why would Stephen and Tessa tell their parents they were going with Penn to his cabin? Then the obvious answer occurred to me.

Stephen and Tessa were off in a motel room somewhere, I thought. Feeling like an idiot, I got in the car and drove back toward town. Penn must be at the library. He had probably forgotten all about his headache and his promise to see me the next day.

But the fright had, like a bad dream, left its mark on me. I wanted to see him, to touch him, to hear for myself that he was all right and that he still loved me. I had to force myself to lighten my foot on the accelerator. My speed was creeping up dangerously.

Penn's house was three stories, with white pillars and a large porch that had been surfaced with terra-cotta tiles. The broad lawn was rimmed with carefully trimmed boxwood hedges and punctuated with tall camellia bushes. Bare branching dogwoods, which were now showing tiny eyelets of leaf, stood over banks of dull-leafed azaleas. The three-car garage was closed, and the morning newspaper lay bound into a roll by a rubber band on the porch. The place seemed to whisper money, tradition, and year-round lawn service.

Wondering what on earth I would say if Penn's father should answer the door, I rang the doorbell. It rang insistently within, but there were no footsteps and no answering call. I banged the brass door knocker, then stabbed the bell once more.

A large envelope stuck out of the white metal mailbox next to the door. It had been folded in half to make it fit. I pulled out the distinctive Express Mail envelope and the top of the mailbox fell shut with a tinny sound. It was addressed to Penn and was from the Bahamian Embassy. As I tore at the flimsy paper I had the sensation of falling down an elevator shaft.

The letter inside was neatly typed. The embassy regretted to inform Penn that workers' permits were not available. I stared at the letter blankly. The Bahamas? My God, I thought. Where is Penn? What is he doing? Why is he asking about workers' permits in the Bahamas?

I drove home in a mental fog, scarcely aware of the traffic. There must be some simple explanation, I told myself. My mind swam with confused images of the Bahamas—traffic officers in white uniforms and pith helmets, old churches built of stone, pink sand.

When I pulled into my driveway, Bobby was hoisting a big black garbage bag with a rattling sound into the trunk of his car. I went inside and fixed myself a cheese sandwich and took an apple out of the fridge. The crunch as I bit into the apple was so painfully loud in my ears that I put it down at once and stared at the clock. "The Bahamas," I told the clock.

I dialed Penn's number again and my heart

stopped when the receiver clicked.

"Hello."

"Hello," I choked out. "Is Penn there?"

"No," a man said. "I'm sorry. He and some friends are out at our cabin this weekend. I'm afraid we don't have a phone out there. Would you care to leave a message?"

"No," I said. "It's not important. I'll call back."

After I hung up, I stared blankly at the refrigerator. The Bahamas? What for?

Twenty

. . . My hand is numb, so is my mind. Not a good day for writing. What's going on? . . .

By Monday morning the rain had returned. It was a sad, cold, plodding rain. In the passageways at school today, kids shook themselves and exclaimed in disgust. They ran, jackets over their heads, across the school grounds and stood shivering together in the corners of classrooms. All day the rain beat a monotonous tattoo as it dripped off the eaves into puddles. I hoped that any minute I would run into Penn or Stephen or Tessa. Surely this would turn out to be one of those merry mix-ups that are cleared up in the last five minutes of a television comedy when it turns out that it is not Miss Murples the receptionist who is having six little ones by a roaming rogue of a fellow but instead Miss Murples's cat. Canned laughter all around. I felt I could use canned laughter, or any kind of laughter at all.

At lunchtime there was no sign of Penn or the others, and my hopes began to shrivel. Reba Rogers sat half-dazed, gazing at a plate of limp pink spaghetti.

"Sorry," I said mechanically when I bumped her chair. She shook herself and blinked.

"So where's Penn?" she asked, peering at me curiously. "I saw he wasn't in history today. Has he got that bug that's going around?"

"I think so," I lied.

"You watch out," she said, "or you're going to get it next."

I planted myself at Nikki's table. Her friends all seemed to be wearing matching navy pleated skirts with navy stockings. It looked like a convention of stewardesses. "I think Penn's got the flu," I said, before any of them had the chance to ask about him.

"A lot of it's going around," said Nikki. "Does he have the kind with the sore throat or the kind with the vomiting and fever?"

"He's got the kind with a bad headache."

"That must be something new," said Nikki respectfully.

Nikki's friends were in the midst of speculating wildly about the romantic lives of their friends. As nearly as I could make out, they were trying to figure all the possible permutations if a girl named Linda finally dumped a guy named Jay. Jay would then chase Jeannette, they presumed, and Jeannette would dump Mark, which meant Suzanne would go after Mark—but I began to lose track. When I had eaten enough spaghetti to stave off starvation, I leapt up from the table, dumped my tray onto the conveyor belt, and charged out of the cafeteria. Unfortunately, I ran right into Casey, the last person I wanted to see. Irrationally, I blamed him for all my problems.

"Where the heck is Penn?" he demanded.

"I don't know," I said.

"What do you mean, you don't know?" He looked taken aback.

Somehow I was not surprised that he knew no more than I did. I couldn't imagine the others' inviting Casey to come along with them to the Bahamas, if that was where they had gone. I wouldn't have invited him anywhere.

He drew his brows together. "I can't find Stephen and Tessa, either. They can't all be out with this stupid flu."

"Maybe they've run away," I said wildly. "Like Laurie. Maybe it's an epidemic of runaways."

"Don't be ridiculous," he snapped.

"I called every one of them over the weekend and their folks said that they'd gone out to the cabin."

"That's it, then," said Casey. "Maybe a road washed out or they ran out of gas or something and got stuck out there in the woods. I knew there had to be some explanation."

"I don't think so. I happened to drive out to the cabin myself on Saturday." I cleared my throat. "And they weren't there. There was no sign of them. And the only tracks on the dirt since the last rain were from my car."

"You're joking," said Casey, the whites of his eyes showing around his irises. "You sound like a detective. So they decided to skip school and go make whoopee. There's no need to make a federal case out of it. You're making a mountain out of a molehill, sweetie pie."

I pursed my lips. "I accept that Stephen and Tessa might be off somewhere making whoopee, as you so quaintly put it. But in that case, where is Penn?"

"With Stephen and Tessa, I bet. Ever heard of a *ménage à trois*?"

I would loved to have wiped that leer off Casey's face with a good sharp slap. His slimy suggestiveness made my flesh creep. "Penn's father believes he's at the cabin," I said icily.

Casey turned his collar up and shivered. "So,

maybe Penn found himself another cutie and they all drove down to the Keys to get some sunshine. I personally wouldn't blame them a bit if they did. This weather stinks."

"Dear Casey." I smiled tightly. "It's always so interesting to get your perspective." I felt a shiver down my spine as I heard myself echoing Tessa's way of speaking. Gone. They had gone without me.

"I call 'em the way I see 'em," Casey said. "Take it from me. Penn won't thank you for raising up a stink about him skipping a day or two of school."

Somehow I got to my classes, but I can't say I noticed much of what went on around me. I stared at the green chalkboards in a trance, thinking "the Bahamas," as if the sheer repetition of the name would yield some answer.

When I got home, I dialed Penn's number. It was not yet four o'clock, and I was startled when Penn's father answered.

"Uh, is Penn home yet?" I asked.

"I'm afraid I missed him last night," Dr. Parrish said. His voice, faintly reminiscent of Penn's, caused a clutch in my heart. "I was up all night with an emergency," he said, "and when I finally got up, Penn had already left for school. Give me your name and I'll leave a note for him on the refrigerator. I'm sure he'll get back to you when he comes in."

I hesitated, flustered, as if I had been asked to take off my mask, but then suddenly gave him my name.

"Ah yes." I could heard the smile in his voice. "Joanna of the red roses."

"Have him call me, please," I said quickly. "Thank you."

When my father came in, he announced that he and Jennifer were off the following day for a vacation in the Caribbean.

"Of course, you've got school so you can't go," he said cheerfully. "But we'll send you a postcard."

I had a vision of a mass exodus to the Caribbean, with everyone in town streaming south, leaving me alone with the monotonous drip of the rain and the shiver of apprehension that ran up my spine.

I had no doubt that Dr. Parrish did as he'd promised and left a note for Penn on the refriger-ator. But Penn hadn't called. And I didn't think he would.

I trudged to school Tuesday wondering how I would manage. The simplest tasks seemed im-possible. I dropped my pencil in physics and stared at the broken point in bewilderment, not quite sure what to do. Getting up to go to the pencil sharpener required more initiative than I could summon. My head ached and I wished I could lie down in a dark room and close my eyes.

On my way to third period, I rounded the corner, and suddenly I saw them, balancing on the brick wall of Eastman—Penn, Tessa, and Stephen. I froze in my tracks for an instant in stunned disbelief. Then I broke into a run and in a minute I was standing before them. Penn grabbed my hands and squeezed them painfully tight. I knew from his touch that whatever was wrong, the problem wasn't between us. Then I met his eyes and I saw that there were dark dents under them. He looked as if he hadn't slept in days.

Casey charged up. "It's about time!" he yelped. "Where've you guys been?"

Tessa and Stephen looked at each other. Their skin seemed to be stretched tight over the fine bones of their faces, and again I saw that eerie echo of one's expression in the face of the other. Their eyes were guarded.

"We had this idea," said Stephen, "that we wanted to see the capital by moonlight."

"It was an impulse," Penn added quickly. "We told our folks we were going to the cabin, but instead we all drove to Washington, D.C."

"And then I said," put in Tessa, "that it wasn't

such a good idea to go to downtown D.C. in the middle of the night, what with the chance we might get mugged, and Penn had this great idea that we would stay over and get up really early and see the sun rise over the Capitol."

"We ended up doing some sight-seeing," said Stephen. "Since we'd come all that way, it seemed too bad to rush back, so we stayed over an extra day."

They were talking quickly, interrupting each other, as if eager to spill their story, but suddenly they all stopped at once.

"Why didn't you ask if I wanted to go?" I cried.

Penn looked at me blankly. "But you're not interested in politics," he said.

I could have burst into laughter if the story hadn't been so absurdly thin. What was the truth? Where had they been? Why were they lying?

"Well, that's great," said Casey crossly, "really great. I've been looking for a shoulder to cry on, and none of you guys was anywhere around. You were off having a good time. Koo dumped me! I caught her making out with Bobby Jenkins!"

Tessa whooped, doubling over in her laughter until it looked as if she might fall backward off the wall. Then she slipped down, gasping for breath.

"I don't see what's so funny," Casey spat.

Penn slid down to Casey's side and banged him on the back. "She's just surprised, aren't you, Tess?"

"Astonished," Tessa choked out.

I half expected Stephen to keel over backward like a bird hit by a BB. He seemed completely shaken and sat on the railing ashen-faced and dazed.

"It's really been rough," said Casey. "You guys can't imagine. I *trusted* her. I thought we really had something there."

"That's bad," said Penn, but the corners of his mouth twitched. "I'm sorry."

"Look at it this way, Casey," said Tessa. "It's her loss."

"Yeah. Easy to say. It's hit me like a ton of bricks," said Casey.

"Time heals the wounds, dear," said Tessa. "Trust me."

"Time wounds all heels," Stephen added, and Tessa shot him a warning look.

"I know it's hard to believe, Casey," Tessa went on, "but you'll look back on this and see it's for the best. Won't he, Penn?"

Penn winced at this allusion to his own fling with Koo, but he recovered quickly. "No joke. You'll be glad, Casey. Just don't look back. Remember that if she behaves that way, she doesn't deserve you."

"Right," said Tessa stoutly.

"On top of it," Casey added, "I lost my car keys somewhere."

I didn't offer an explanation.

After everyone had commiserated with Casey on his misfortune, Penn walked with me to my homeroom in silence. "You seem awfully quiet this morning," he said finally. "Are you okay?"

"I was worried about you," I cried. "I thought maybe you'd keeled over dead. I went over to your house. I even drove out to the cabin."

He bit his lip. "I'm sorry. I didn't think you'd want to go with us."

We had reached the door to my homeroom. "I picked up your mail while I was over at your house. I couldn't help looking at it. You heard from the Bahamian Embassy," I said flatly. "I saved the letter for you, but the gist of it, if you're interested, is that you don't have a hope of getting a work permit."

His light-colored eyes were troubled.

"Don't you want to comment on that?" I asked.

"No." He shook his head ruefully. "I think I'll let it lie."

I pulled away from him and pressed through the crowd toward the door.

"Joanna, I'll call you!" he said, raising his voice to be heard.

The school day was a total loss. The fluorescent lights that buzzed over my head made it sound like a particularly annoying insect was at large. The shuffle of sneakers on gritty floor, the monotony of the teachers' voices, the boring intricacies of calculus, history, and physics offered no real competition for the drama in my mind. If Penn loved me, how could he treat me this way? I had spent a miserable three days wondering what had become of him, with no one to turn to. He could have called. No matter what was going on—and I was sure that he had not driven five hours in order to see the capital by moonlight— still he could have called me and let me know where he was.

I thought of Bobby and how he had not heard from Laurie since she left weeks ago. For the first time I felt some sympathy for Bobby's wild violence. He must be sick with worry. He must be counting over every word he ever said to her and wondering what could justify her treating him in such a way. How could she have abandoned him?

When I got home after school, I glanced at myself in the bathroom mirror and saw that my eyes were unnaturally bright. My head ached, and the floor felt unsteady, as if I were on a pitching boat. My bedroom was dim, which was good, since light hurt my eyes. The blinds were closed and there was no light except for the lamp on my night table, which I flicked off. I felt very unsteady, so I sat down on the side of the bed. I wondered if this was what it felt like to die. In the last minutes of life perhaps the world shifted underfoot and then faded away into darkness.

Suddenly the doorbell rang. It must be a delivery for my father, I thought, touching my hand gingerly to my head. If I just sit here, they'll go away. But the doorbell rang insistently, and at last I struggled to my feet. I walked like a drunk person, brushing the walls on either side of the hall with my outstretched fingertips.

This must be an effect of stress, I told myself. Either that or I'm coming down with something. I cracked the door open cautiously. It was Penn.

"Joanna," he said, alarmed. "You look awful." He came in.

"Thanks. Actually, I feel kind of awful." I swallowed and my knees seemed to give way.

Penn caught me. "Which room is yours?" he asked, but it seemed too much trouble to answer and I leaned my head against his chest and let tears stream down my cheeks. He lifted me off my feet, carrying me in his arms. I could hear my breath whistling against his shirt and feel my heart pounding in my ears. I was so tired, more tired than I could remember being before. The walls of the room seemed to be moving and my head hurt.

He tucked me into my bed. Worry shadowed his brow. "Do you have any idea what's wrong?" he asked.

"Stress," I said, licking my lips. "I have had a lot of stress in my life lately."

"Who's your regular doctor?" he asked.

"Excuse me," I said. I jumped up, pushed him out of my way, ran into the bathroom, and threw up into the toilet. Afterward I felt much better. I wiped a wet washcloth over my mouth and staggered back to the bed.

"Looks like it's the flu," said Penn.

I groaned. "I feel terrible."

"When is your dad getting in?"

I tried to remember and couldn't. Then it came to me. "He's not coming in," I said. "He's in the Caribbean. He's taking a vacation."

Penn uttered a short expletive.

"I'll be okay," I said. "I already feel a lot better. I'm just going to lie here and go to sleep." I was shaking with chills now and pulled the cover up to my chin.

My dreams were horrifying. Pea-green men had kidnapped me and were holding me captive in a square house on a road that somehow led to the Caribbean. When I woke up, the room was spinning. I staggered to the bathroom and retched again. Penn wiped my face off and said he was going to run home and get some medicine. When he got back, I took some pills in tiny cellophane packages. They may have helped. I'm not sure. I began to lose track of time.

Laurie's face swam in my brain so vividly and insistently, I thought maybe I was beginning to hallucinate. It was hard for me to think straight. The yellow rubber gloves Stephen had bought appeared in my dream. They had come to life and were grabbing and holding Laurie as she screamed. Her open mouth was like a black hole in her face. There was something dreadfully obscene about the rubber gloves, but I wasn't sure what it was, only that it was frightening and I was running away, running with all my might.

When I woke up, my skin was clammy and damp. My nightgown was sticking to me and I stumbled out of bed to change into another one. It seemed as if I had been sick forever. I remembered vaguely a healthy world in which people worked, played basketball, and acted in plays. It seemed incredible anyone would have that kind of energy. I tried to lie very still in some position that didn't hurt too much.

Sometimes when I woke from my feverish

sleep, I became conscious of Penn standing quietly by the bed, and in that half-consciousness between sleep and waking everything seemed simple. There was only him and me and this sick feeling, and if I ever got over feeling sick, everything would be okay.

Penn brought me clear chicken soup, dry salty crackers, and an endless supply of cool wet washcloths.

"Feel like sitting up yet?" he asked, propping pillows behind me.

To my surprise, I did.

He pulled up the blinds, and I was amazed to see it was sunny out. I had been living in a perpetual twilight unaware of morning and evening. I couldn't have said with any certainty at all whether it was night or day. But sunlight glinted off of the pond outside. There was a flurry of wings as three mallard ducks flew in, their orange feet stretched out before them, and braked for a landing on the pond. They landed with a noisy splash.

"How long have you been here?" I asked.

"A couple days."

"But what about school?"

"I phoned in and told them I had this terrible bug that's going around. Then I told my father I had to look out for a sick friend. Stephen's been bringing by my homework. I've been getting a fair amount done. Amazing how much time you can save by not going to school."

"You probably saved my life," I said.

He grinned. "Hold on to that thought. I get off on abject gratitude. When you're a little better, you may kiss my feet."

"Seriously."

"Seriously, it wasn't as bad as that. You probably would have gotten a little more dehydrated than you did, but I doubt it would have been fatal. The human body is tougher than you'd think." His face clouded. "Though in other ways it's not so tough."

"Penn." I gripped the bedspread in wadded-up handfuls in my palm, as if I expected the bed to begin to buck. "Why were you—trying to get away?" There was no hiding the hurt in my voice, and I didn't even try.

"I'm sorry," he said softly.

"Laurie's dead, isn't she?" I said.

He froze and looked at me with a completely expressionless face. He looked like a wax mask of his face. But I didn't need him to tell me Laurie was dead. I knew she must be.

"That's why Bobby hasn't heard from her." I clasped my hands together tightly. "That was the only reason I could think of why she wouldn't have gotten in touch with Bobby.

What have you done? Why were you trying to get permits to work in the Bahamas? Did you— kill her?"

Looking at him, I felt so cold that I could have been a sculpture chipped out of ice.

Twenty-one

. . . I almost wish my fever would come back, that I could toss in bed too hot and dizzy and dazed to concentrate on what I had just heard . . .

Penn made a gesture as if he were pushing away my question. He got the yellow armchair that faced the television and brought it over beside my bed. Then he sat down, resting his elbows on his knees and letting his hands fall between his legs and looked at me soberly. "No, I didn't kill her. Would it make any difference if I did?"

I thought about it. "Yes," I said. "It would have to make a difference, wouldn't it? It would mean you were different from who I thought you were."

"Now you're scaring me," he said heavily. "Look, I didn't kill her. Maybe we'd better leave it at that."

"If you had only called me before you left town," I cried. If only he had told me he would be away, I realized, I would have gone on seeing nothing beyond the pleasant surface Penn and Stephen and Tessa presented to the world. I wished it had happened that way.

"I didn't want you to get dragged into it," Penn said. "We're all in so deep it's hopeless. But not you. You're okay."

"No," I said. "I'm in deep, too. It's too late to leave me out of it. You have to tell me." My voice sounded strange even to my own ears. I had the sensation the walls were closing in on me, and there was a sick feeling in the pit of my stomach. I leaned back. It was very possible that I wasn't quite over the flu. Either that, or I was more horrified than I had ever been.

There was a long silence, and finally he said, "Where do you want me to start?"

"Tell me what happened."

"Maybe I'd better begin at the beginning. Remember when Casey said my driver's license was clean?"

"Yes."

"You said you were surprised. How surprised were you?"

I remembered the day in The Bakery when Casey had teased Penn about his perfectly clean driving record. I had driven with Penn. Why hadn't I realized how impossible it would be for a driver so in love with speed to have a clean record?

"Casey wasn't fooling when he said he broke into the Department of Motor Vehicles' computer, was he?" I said.

He smiled. "I told you I admired your mind. You've got it right on the button."

The slanted light from the window made sculptured snowy heaps out of the disordered bedclothes. The china lamp on my bedside table cast a violin-shaped shadow onto the wall. My fingers worked, clutching at the sheets aimlessly.

"So Casey cleaned up your driving record for you?" I said. I hardly recognized my own voice.

Penn nodded. "I was close to losing my license, and I was scared. Casey said it'd be a piece of cake to take care of it. He knew how to do it."

"And you said, 'Oh, no, Casey. Don't do that because I believe in equal treatment under the law.'"

"I wish." Penn coughed as he glanced at me uneasily. "I need to get some water," he said. He stood up quickly. "Hang on a minute."

I had so many questions to ask him, I couldn't

think how to begin. I was dizzy, disoriented, as if my entire world had been set spinning. I heard cabinets opening and closing in the kitchen and then the heaviness of his footfall on the carpet in the hall.

Penn hesitated a moment in the doorway, the slanted light falling on his face. I found myself remembering the moment his car had sped out of control and we found ourselves looking at the guardrail only inches away from the sheer drop that would have meant our deaths. His face had been as bleached then as it was now. It occurred to me that for him speed was like pepper on the food of an old alcoholic who no longer has a sense of taste. Since his mother had left and even more since Laurie had died, he had made himself numb to so much that it was very possible he needed speed to make him feel anything at all. The thought made me faintly ill.

Penn placed his glass of water on my bedside table and sat down again in the yellow chair. There was a crease between his eyebrows, but he was as calm as if he were about to explain a particularly tricky physics problem.

"What happened after Casey fixed your driver's license?" I asked. "Did he really break into NASA's computer? Have you been selling government secrets or something? Is that why you always have plenty of cash?"

He looked surprised. "Are you serious?"

I sagged against the pillows. "Just an idea. What happened, then?"

"You know how set Stephen is on being a National Merit Scholar and on going to Princeton? Well, when he was in the ninth grade, he got a C in English. The teacher had it in for him and gave him a rotten grade on his research paper. Stephen was afraid that might really sink him. It would probably have stopped him from being a National Merit Scholar. Anyway, Casey said he could change the C to an A."

"A regular little miracle worker, Casey, isn't he?" I said. "I'm beginning to see why everybody finds him so charming. You can forgive a guy a lot when it turns out he can clean up your whole life by pushing a few buttons."

Penn flushed. "Maybe it was out of line for him to mess with my driving record, but what he did for Stephen was perfectly okay. You know how subjective grades are. Stephen should have gotten at least a B in that course. He's smart and he kills himself working. That teacher had it in for him."

"I'm surprised Casey is still worried about getting into MIT," I said. "He could change all his grades to A's and he'd be in like that." I snapped my fingers.

"Not really. There's a limit to what he

could do without anybody's noticing. It's one thing to change a single grade that Stephen got four years ago; it's something else again for it to turn out suddenly on Monday morning that Casey has come up since Friday from twentieth in the class to valedictorian. Somebody would be bound to notice." Penn gave me a sideways glance. "Are you thinking all kinds of grim puritanical things? You've got that kind of look."

I felt my ears grow warm. "I don't mean to be that way," I said. "I can see how being able to break into computers would be a big temptation." I thought how silent Tessa and Stephen had been in the car that day when I said I had heard Casey was a computer whiz. Why hadn't I known something was wrong?

"Maybe I ought to stop there," said Penn ruefully. "It gets worse."

"Laurie found out about it?" I asked.

"How did you guess?" He looked at me under his lashes. "Not that it was any deep secret. I mean, Laurie was the only one of us who didn't know the whole story, but she was having so much trouble at home, and she'd gotten so deep into this weird thing with Bobby."

I remembered Bobby's puzzled grief that Laurie had left without saying a word. One day they had been lovers and the next she was gone.

"I guess you think Bobby is pretty awful," I said slowly.

"Sure I do." Penn was surprised. "You know he is. You've met him."

"He's not so bad," I said, looking away from him uncomfortably.

"I figured Laurie hung out with him in order to drive her mother crazy," said Penn. "Mrs. J. wanted Bobby to stay away. She kept screaming, calling Laurie names. Laurie was coming apart. That was another thing—" He hesitated.

"You weren't sure how much you could trust Laurie since she was freaking out."

He shrugged. "It's just that we sort of figured she had enough to handle as it was. Why give her something else to worry about?"

I swallowed. "Go ahead. What happened?"

"It was on the thirteenth." He smiled sadly. "Unlucky number."

"That was a few days before I got to town."

"I guess it was."

I recalled how surprised the others had been that Penn had asked me to go along to The Bakery with them. They must have been aching to talk privately. Their nerviness on that occasion seemed all too understandable, now that I looked back. The amazing thing was that they had managed to keep up the charade, pretending nothing was wrong.

Penn lifted his head, looking out the window at the lake and the skidding ducks. A semicircle of light gleamed in his pupils, giving his eyes a curious blankness. "We were having some great weather that day," he said. "The sky was perfectly blue. The sun was shining. We decided to do a picnic up at Lookout Point. Laurie rode over with me in the 'Vette."

My pulse was racing. Suddenly I was afraid of what he would say next.

He glanced at me. "I got stopped by a cop. Laurie was surprised I wasn't more upset about the ticket. She kept carrying on about what it would do to my insurance rates. She said she was surprised I hadn't lost my license by now." Penn rubbed his nose. "She always was high-strung."

"But you didn't tell her your little secret."

"No, I wasn't that crazy." He hesitated. "I don't know. Maybe I should have said something after all, because when I kept quiet, it seemed to make her more hysterical. She was getting into full gear by the time we got to the picnic table. I started unpacking the stuff, but Laurie kept at me. She had the idea something strange was going on, and she wouldn't let go of it. I tried to tune her out, but Casey—" He stopped abruptly.

Holding my breath, I stared, waiting for him to go on.

"Casey couldn't stop himself from bragging," he said at last.

"So, he told her how he'd fixed your license. I guess he told her how he'd changed Stephen's grade, too."

"Yeah. He even asked her if there was anything he could do for her! He was showing off," said Penn bitterly. "He couldn't seem to stop himself. Of course, he had no idea Laurie was going to be so weird about it. I've thought about everything that happened a hundred times since then. I mean, we were all surprised Laurie was so wrought up. She was acting like we were up for *America's Most Wanted* or something. I couldn't figure out why it was such a big deal to her. I wonder if maybe she wasn't mad because we could fix up our troubles at the computer while her troubles were dragging her under." He made a helpless gesture.

"So what happened?"

"It was an accident, actually. You know, Stephen's got kind of a short fuse." He paused uncomfortably.

As if the memory were burned in my mind, I could picture Casey teasing Stephen about his short temper and the white look of Stephen's face.

Penn glanced at me and went on. "When Laurie started spitting all these accusations out at him and threatening to go public and make sure he never got any kind of scholarship much less accepted at Princeton, he was furious. They got to shoving each other. The rest of us were so shocked that I don't think we even gave a thought to how close they were to the edge of the overlook. Then suddenly the ground sort of gave way at the edge—Laurie lost her balance and went over." Penn's face was ghostly. "It was bad. Stephen said, 'Laurie?' in this kind of puzzled way, like he hadn't expected her to disappear so fast. I can still hear him saying it sometimes at night when I'm trying to get to sleep." He shook his head as if trying to clear it of the memory. "Then he made a move to try to go down after her. Well, at that, Tessa threw her arms around him and got hysterical. We were all still thinking that maybe Laurie had only broken an arm or something, I don't know. We really couldn't see that well from where we were, and nobody much wanted to get close to the edge now that we saw it wasn't that stable." He shrugged hopelessly. "So we all jumped in Stephen's car and drove down the road and then up to that parking place near the falls. I think I still expected her to walk out of the bushes and say boo." He looked puzzled. "You know, it's amazingly hard to think of somebody as dead when they've been alive a minute or two before."

"You found her?"

"Yeah. The river was so low, you know, all the rocks were exposed all over the place. If it hadn't been such a dry year, the water might have broken her fall." He frowned. "Of course, it's a heck of a drop. But you hear now and then about people jumping off the Golden Gate Bridge, even, and living to tell the tale."

"Not often."

"No. But this wasn't as big a drop as the Golden Gate Bridge, either. It was certainly possible that it might not have killed her. We went along the bank a ways and then we saw her, lying on the rocks in the water. We all waded out there, calling her name."

I remembered Tessa's nausea, her worry about what crayfish eat. How she must be haunted by the memory of Laurie's broken body lying limp on the rocks.

Penn turned his palms upward helplessly. "She was dead. Her neck was broken, not to mention there must have been some pretty severe internal injuries." He pulled a handkerchief out of his pocket and blotted his lips. "I put my hands under her arms and Stephen got her legs and we carried her over to the shore. That's how I know her neck was broken. It . . . wasn't right." He hesitated. "Of course, we were pretty much in shock. Later on, I kept asking myself if we should have left her there and driven off. It might have looked like a suicide." He folded the handkerchief carefully and put it back in his pocket. "But there's no use thinking of that. There's no way we could have done it. You see, we'd all been friends since we were kids. There was no way we could have left her out there on the rocks."

"But if it was an accident, surely—"

Penn shook his head. "We should have gone to the police and taken our chances. We should have left her where she was and hoped it would pass for suicide. We should have done anything but what we did. But we were scared. Here Laurie had been carrying on about what criminals we were! So Tessa, who got remarkably clearheaded all of a sudden, adrenaline I guess, pointed out that if there was a serious investigation, it might come out that three of us had motives to kill her."

"Three of you?"

"Think about it—Stephen, Casey, and me. Tessa, too, if you figure she'd do anything to protect Stephen, which in fact she would. The only reason we got away with fiddling with my driver's record and Stephen's grades was because nobody was watching us. Nobody really expects high-school students to be up to something like that.

We're supposed to be too busy with our homework and not half bright, anyway." He smiled faintly. "If the police started poking around thinking Laurie had been murdered, they might have turned up what we'd done. It was entirely possible we could have been tried and convicted. I can see the headlines now. 'Teen Computer Gang Murders Classmate.' 'Honor Students' Thrill Kill.'"

"So what did you do?"

"We dragged her out of the water and kept checking for a pulse and hoping that she'd suddenly start to breathe, but she must have died instantly. We were in a panic." He shook his head. "We started out on a picnic and we ended up with a dead body. It's no wonder we weren't acting all that rational."

"I guess you had to go back and get the picnic things."

"Tessa remembered that, too. Believe me, it was the last thing on my mind. But you're right. We had to go back and clean up all signs of the picnic. I haven't much cared for spiced steamed shrimp since then."

I recalled Tessa once pushing away shrimp that had been brought by mistake at a restaurant and her lame explanation. One of the many little incongruities I had closed my eyes to.

"Then came the hard part," Penn said. "We

had to go home and act like nothing had happened. When Laurie's mom called and asked if we had seen her, we had to be real low key and act like everything was normal, and all the time we're wrecks. Particularly once the police came around asking questions. When you have as much on your conscience as we did, having a couple of uniformed cops show up at your house can about finish you. When they talked to me, I had this awful feeling that I was babbling. I must have looked guilty as sin."

"I can see that talking to the police would be tricky," I said. My lips felt numb. What about Laurie's mother? I thought. What about Bobby? Both of them had been crazy with grief that Laurie had abruptly vanished. I had to remind myself forcefully that Penn and the others had been terrified. That was why they had focused only on their own survival. It was only human.

"It turns out the first thing Laurie's mother thought," Penn said, "was that Laurie'd committed suicide. She'd been acting weepy and upset, you see. It didn't occur to us until then that if we had let her be, it could have passed for suicide. Of course, if we'd gone that route, we would have had to come up with some way she could have gotten up to the overlook by herself, because she didn't have her own car."

"Just as well that she didn't," I said. "You'd have had to get rid of it somehow when you decided to make it look as if she ran away." With a queer start, I realized I was thinking like Penn and the others.

"Right. And we had to do that."

I had the vaguely uncomfortable feeling that I had stepped over a line and that there was no going back. I had quit sitting in judgment on my friends. Almost imperceptibly I had moved to Penn's side. I wasn't sure how, but something vital had shifted.

"You can see that it was absolutely crucial that we get rid of the cops," Penn went on. "It was bad enough when they were dragging the lake behind the school and we had to pretend to be worried they were going to pull up her body."

"The looking-worried part must have come easy," I said.

"I guess." Penn lifted his water glass and drank. "But you get to where you don't know what's natural, you're so self-conscious. Every breath you take feels phony. You get to where you can't remember how normal people swallow or how often they blink. And it was worse when they didn't find her in the lake and the cops started coming around to our houses asking more questions. Every one of us had to worry that one of the others was cracking and spilling the beans. We were nervous wrecks. If it kept up, it was perfectly possible that somebody actually would snap and then we would all end up in prison. So we had to get rid of the cops. That's why we decided to have Laurie write her mom." He wearily leaned his elbows on his knees, letting his hands dangle.

"Some trick." My eyes were drawn to his long slender fingers with the heavy class ring winking gravely, a point of light in the shadow cast by my bed. I could see how the others must have depended on Penn. Looking back, I realized that Stephen and Tessa had been on the verge of breaking for weeks. From my present vantage point, Tessa's bright remark "All for one and one for all!" that first day at The Bakery sounded like an anxious plea. She must have been desperate that the group hold firm.

"It wasn't that hard," Penn said, "since nobody really thought Laurie'd been murdered. It's not as if the police gave the letter a big workover to see if it was genuine. Everybody simply assumed it was. I typed it on an ancient Underwood typewriter that I found in our garage, and then I traced Laurie's signature off the Christmas card she gave me. It took me a few tries, but the final result was good enough to fool just about anybody."

"It must have been a big relief to her

mother to hear from her," I said dryly.

Penn sucked in his breath. "I'm not saying we deserve the Good Citizen of the Year Award, but keep in mind that we were scared out of our wits. We felt like we had to do something to get the police out of the picture. Remember that first day we went to The Bakery together, how I had to leave early?"

I nodded.

"I drove straight to D.C. and mailed the letter from there."

I remembered Penn's hurry to get away that day. No wonder Tessa's eyes had followed Penn's car so anxiously as he drove away. With Stephen in danger, Penn's errand must have seemed to her both desperate and risky.

"Of course, I had to be careful not to get a speeding ticket," Penn said, "but I have the only really reliable car, and I can make the best time, so it made sense for me to do it. I tried to make it look as if it was a normal sort of day and then I drove up there and back, eight hours round trip, without stopping except for gas. The idea was that nobody would even notice I had been gone."

I remembered my surprise at the huge number of miles he had put on his odometer. "So did you ask me to The Bakery to have an impartial witness to this so-called normal day?"

"Nah." He ran a finger gently along my arm. "Come on, Joanna. You know it wasn't that way. It's such a relief to be telling you about it. It's been grim bottling all this stuff up. Time and again, I wanted to spill everything, but it didn't seem fair to drag you into it."

I swallowed. "Well, so once you mailed the letter, then your troubles were over, huh?"

"Not exactly," said Penn ruefully. "We hadn't thought it all out. We left Laurie's body right there on the bank of the river while we tried to figure out what to do. The falls were dry, and with it being winter, hardly anybody was going out to the park. She was pretty well hidden with all the bushes on the shore there. Not that we had planned it. It just turned out that way." He shrugged. "Then we started thinking that when she was found, nobody would ever link her death to us because by the time they found her, nobody would even be able to tell exactly when she'd died. But when those guys at school started talking about how we pretty much had dibs on that picnic table at the overlook, Stephen started to lose it. If they found her any-time soon, it was going to be pretty obvious from the nature of the injuries that she had fallen from the overlook. The way Stephen looked at it, that pointed right to us. With all the rain and the flooding, it seemed pretty inevitable that she was going to be found soon. There was even a chance the river would flood enough to sweep her body off the bank and back into the water. She was right about where those guys in the canoe capsized. They had cops and rescue personnel all over the place, what with those guys out hanging on to a tree and the missing campers and all."

I recalled everyone's preoccupation with the rain, Stephen and Tessa's panic at the word the river might flood. "But they didn't find her, did they?" I was puzzled.

Penn sucked on his lower lip a second, and then spoke. "No. Because we moved her."

"You moved her?" I said stupidly.

"That was the worst part."

"Is that why Stephen was buying three pairs of rubber gloves?" I asked slowly.

"Yeah."

My stomach heaved. Those nightmares about the yellow gloves coming alive—some part of me must have known those three pairs of rubber gloves were sinister. Nobody needed three pairs of gloves for refinishing furniture. Stephen's white face swam before my eyes. He had been shaken when I appeared unexpectedly that night in the drugstore and had caught him preparing for his grim task. Now his panic seemed perfectly understandable.

Penn went on. "We went down to the river with flashlights—it was fairly risky, actually, with the water so high—and we rolled her body onto a plastic tarp and put it in the trunk of Stephen's car. We used Stephen's car because it was so ordinary looking."

"Is that why Stephen burned up his car?"

Penn nodded. "He was going crazy thinking of how there would be bound to be traces of the body in the trunk if the police forensic people ever started going over it. So we decided it had to be completely destroyed. But it had to look like an accident, of course."

I remembered how we had gone out to the cabin the weekend the water rose, and Penn had laughed helplessly when Casey had proclaimed himself an advocate of law and order. Stephen had arrived and collapsed on the sofa weak and sick to his stomach while Tessa regarded him anxiously. No wonder he had recovered so quickly from the "flu." He hadn't had the flu at all, just a bad case of physical revulsion after the gruesome task of disposing of Laurie's body.

"The trick," Penn said, "was to take the body someplace that had no connection with us. If you think about it a minute, you'll see how hard it would be to come up with a place like that. All the places you can think of that might be good places to hide bodies turn out to be places you know pretty well. That means they could be easily connected with you."

I noticed that Penn's need to maintain a smooth surface still held strong. His every word was layered by an artificial tone of calm reasonableness, as if he were solving a math problem.

"Luckily," he went on, "Tessa had the idea of getting a government ordinance map, one of those things that marks practically every tree and pebble in the area of a few miles or so. She photocopied the one the library had and then left the photocopy in Stephen's car the night it burned. That's how we found the place we used. We went up an old logging road—it was overgrown and we were lucky to get the car through without any damage. We carried Laurie off into the trees and rolled her out off the tarp. Then we covered the body with pine straw and leaves."

I wiped my sweaty palms on the bedspread. "If Stephen wanted to move the body, I don't see why he and Tessa couldn't have done it," I said. "There wasn't any reason for you to get involved."

"All for one and one for all," he said.

Penn's eyes shifted, and in that flashing instant the slight movement and a quiver in the mobile line of his mouth showed me the struggle he felt. His careless love of speed and his loyalty to his friends had led him inch by inch down a path of destruction. He had moved instinctively to protect his friends. How could I blame him for it? I loved him. And I needed him desperately.

"I'm the one with the strongest stomach," Penn continued slowly. "We weren't all that sure that Stephen wouldn't pass out when it came time to move the body. Then what would Tessa have done? We'd had fairly cold weather, but the body was exposed and Laurie'd gotten," he looked uncomfortable, "soft."

The doorbell buzzed insistently, and I gazed at Penn in wild alarm.

Twenty-two

Dear Diary,
Well, now I'm initiated. No longer an outsider. It's what I wanted, right? To share secrets with a boyfriend, with friends. But I didn't think it would be this way. . . .

Stephen and Tessa burst into the bedroom, grinning broadly. Tessa was clutching a quart jar of a milky, yellowish liquid. Stephen tossed his hair back with a jerk and sniffled noisily. He was gingerly holding a casserole dish beaded with moisture on the outside and being careful not to dump the bunch of bananas that were perched precariously on its lid.

"Where can we put this stuff?" Tessa asked. "The pudding ought to go in the fridge. All the best for what ails you, my dear. Chicken soup, tapioca pudding, easily digestible bananas. Food for the invalid."

"Let's take it to the kitchen," said Penn hastily.

"You look terrible," said Tessa, staring at me. "Like you've seen a ghost." She put the jar of chicken soup down on top of the television. "I thought you'd be over it by now. Are you still running a fever?"

I suppose the horror of what I had heard was written all over my face, because when I didn't speak and looked first at her and then at Stephen, Tessa went ashen. She swallowed hard. "You didn't, Penn."

Penn shrugged. "She guessed."

The bunch of bananas slid to the floor. Stephen froze, standing there with the casserole dish.

"Put it down, Stephen," snapped Tessa.

He placed the dish carefully on the floor. "I think I may faint," he said.

"Sit down, then," said Tessa.

He sat down cross-legged behind the casserole dish. "Did you?" He stared at me unblinking. "Did you guess, I mean?"

I nodded.

"Damn!" cried Stephen. "Everybody must know."

"Calm down!" Penn ordered. "It's all right."

"Sure," I said weakly. "Besides, what's done is done."

"It was an accident," said Stephen, his eyes pleading with me.

"I know that," I said. But a doubt like a trickle of ice water ran through me. "Of course it was," I said. "It's over and done with."

"You can see why we got scared when Casey got so tight with Koo," said Stephen. "Tessa was afraid he'd brag to her, and believe me, Koo is not one you could trust to keep her mouth shut."

"That was when I wrote to the Bahamian Embassy," Penn said. "You see, we figured we needed a place to bolt to if Casey blabbed. I don't know, it seems incredibly stupid now, but we panicked. All of a sudden Casey's running with the fast crowd, and then you tell me he's gotten wasted and is chattering away about the computers he broke into, including NASA's. What if somebody called the FBI?"

"Penn still hadn't heard from the Bahamian Embassy," Tessa put in, "even though he sent everything Express Mail, so we took off. Our plan was to present ourselves there Monday morning and find out about the work permits. If everything was systems go, we could catch a boat right out of D.C. But as you know, we couldn't get permits."

"I would have been lonesome here without you," I said bleakly.

Tessa shot me a brilliant smile.

Penn squeezed my hand. "Don't worry, we're never going to leave you," he said.

A very tight clique, Nikki had said, not knowing how true her words were. Now, indisputably I belonged to it, bound by the ties not only of affection but of guilt. How would I be able to look Bobby in the eye again, knowing what I knew? Yet I was certain that I would. I would carry it off because I had to.

Penn kissed me.

"Watch out," said Stephen. "You may catch that flu."

Penn smiled. "Heck, Joanna and I share everything."

I held his hand tightly.

Penn whispered in my ear. "I love you."

His hand was warm in mine. I half-closed my teary eyes and saw Tessa and Stephen blur into the pastel shades of flowers, spring, and sunshine. Outside, I heard a splash and the hoarse cry of a solitary heron.

Epilogue

Dear Diary,

I thought that was the end of the story, but it was really only the beginning. An image began to repeat in my head that I was powerless to stop. A girl is falling, clawing at the air, her mouth open, her eyes wide in terror. She seems to fall for a long time. Then, with a splash, she strikes the rocks of a riverbed and her head snaps to an unnatural angle.

I've done a lot of looking back since that afternoon. I've asked myself many times if this story could have been different, but try as I might, I can't envision it any other way. Could I have walked away from Penn? Could I have refused to get involved? Could I even, perhaps, have turned all four of them in to the police?

But I couldn't do that. I loved Penn.

And even as the image of Laurie's death stayed like a sliver of ice in my heart, another scene came to haunt me—Stephen drawing three concentric circles on the door of the old outhouse at the cabin. The central circle, crosshatched with black pen to make a bull's-eye, drew my eye as if it held the secret of my future.

Don't miss BETRAYAL,
the next book in this
thrilling series.

Dear Diary,

"I love Penn Parrish." I wrote that weeks ago. It's true now more than ever. But I'm scared, Diary. I wake up at three in the morning with the shakes, my skin clammy. While I was sick with the flu, Penn told me something terrible, and ever since, I've been having the same nightmare over and over. In it a girl is falling, clawing at the air, her mouth open, her eyes wide in terror. She seems to fall for a long time. Then she strikes the rocks of the riverbed with a thud, and her head snaps to an unnatural angle. She lies there, face to the sky, and the shallow water moves her wispy hair.

The worst part is waking up. Then I realize that the nightmare is real. Laurie Jenkins is dead.

*   *   *

For years I've written my diary in code. It's something I started in the sixth grade, when I thought my parents were spying on me. Stupid. But now I'm glad my diary is secret. If it weren't, I could never write the truth. It would be far too dangerous.

Saturday morning my father was snoring in his room at the back of the house. He had come back sunburned from a Caribbean vacation, bringing with him painted coconuts and a floppy hat made of woven palm fronds. I might have felt jealous of his vacation if I hadn't been so excited about spending the weekend at Penn's cabin out in the woods. The entire gang would be there, and it was good to be included. But what made my heart beat hard and made me press my cold hand against my suddenly flushed cheeks was the thought that I would be with Penn.

Noticing my hand was trembling, I put down my cup of cocoa. On the pond outside, a mallard reared, quacking angrily, and then settled back on the water in a flutter of ruffled feathers. I could see the few golf carts that were already out on the golf course. In the distance they darted, beetlelike, by the orange flag fluttering over the green.

A few muffin crumbs floated on the surface of the greasy water in the kitchen sink. I turned away, feeling weak in the knees. It's because I've just gotten over the flu, I told myself. That's all.

I opened the living-room window, and suddenly I heard the roar of Penn's Corvette. It seemed to take a long time to get my overnight bag. It was odd that my heart was racing, but my legs refused to respond. I pushed the door open and grasped the handle of the bag. "I'm all right," I said aloud. "I'm only tired."

I saw the red convertible pulling into the driveway. Stumbling down the steps, I let my overnight bag fall from my grasp as I watched the car door open. Sunshine picked out platinum strands in Penn's ash-blond hair and gave it fire. *Beautiful!* I thought, catching my breath suddenly. I wanted to cradle his head in my hands and kiss him. I imagined us walking on the beach, picking wildflowers and drinking champagne like lovers in a corny movie. I suppose I must have been woozy, because for a fraction of a second that plan seemed practical. He put his hands on either side of my waist. "Are you okay?" he asked. "You're so pale."

I grinned foolishly—the sight of him had that effect on me. "Just the postviral blahs."

"You'd better take it easy. How was your father's vacation?" It was Penn who had nursed me through the flu while my father was having fun in the islands. Dad had an uncanny knack for disappearing whenever I needed him.

"He did some snorkeling," I said, "got sunburned, and drank margaritas. That was about all he told me." Penn opened the door for me, and I fell against the soft leather of the bucket seat. "I wonder if I'll ever see this Jennifer person he goes out with," I said.

The car backed slowly out of the driveway. Then Penn pressed his foot down firmly on the accelerator, as if he had been granted lifetime immunity from speed limits. "Maybe she doesn't even exist," he said. "Maybe all the time your dad says he's with her, he's really curled up with a set of blueprints."

"Maybe he's lying to her about his age," I said. "He might not want to let on that he's old enough to have a seventeen-year-old daughter. I'll bet that's why he's not bringing her around."

At the side of the main road a man in a business suit stood next to a German shepherd that was lying on the ground. My hand went to my mouth. There was a loud buzzing in my ears. The dog was breathing, but his middle was flat.

"Don't look," said Penn, speeding past.

I gasped for breath. I could still see the dog, even though my eyes were now closed.

"Are you all right?" Penn's hand rested on my knee.

I felt dizzy. "Yes, I'll be okay in a minute," I insisted.

I let my head drop back against the seat. The

music from the car radio began to blend with the hum of the car's engine and with Penn's voice. . . . A videotape had begun in my head that I was powerless to stop. In it, a girl is falling, clawing at the air, her mouth open, her eyes wide in terror. It was the familiar nightmare.

"Knock-knock-knocking on heaven's door," sang a monotonous whine on the radio. I jerked suddenly, startled by the sound.

"You were falling asleep," Penn said. He tossed me his jacket. "Here, use this for a pillow."

I shook my head. "No. I'm awake." I was afraid of what I might dream if I fell asleep. But even with my eyes wide open and focused on the road ahead of us, the images and noises in my head would not stop. . . . There is a crackling sound as the girl's body, soft at the surface, like Jell-O, is rolled by rubber-gloved hands onto a black plastic tarp. The long black bundle is lifted and awkwardly jackknifed until it will fit in a car trunk. The trunk slams shut with a whoosh of air and the solid sound of metal meeting metal.

The car, its lights turned low, bumps precariously along a deserted logging road, striking stones and fallen tree limbs as it goes. At last it stops, and dark figures pull the bundled tarp out of the trunk. They breathe heavily with fear and with the effort needed for their grisly task. "Be careful," cries a familiar voice. Dry branches break, and the dead leaves of the forest crack and crumble under their feet. They lower their morbid burden to the ground, then roll the softening body out onto the leaves. They frantically bunch up the black plastic tarp. With their bare hands looking like flashes of white in the light reflected from the night sky, they scoop up handfuls of leaves and throw them on top of the body. "Let's get out of here," says a panicked whisper. Tossed leaves fall gently and an open white hand lying on the ground the last trace of the body, disappears. "I feel sick," says a voice.

"You can't be sick now," someone responds. The little car's motor coughs as it goes back the way it came, bumping over obstacles in the abandoned road.

Funny thing. The next image is less vivid, though this was the scene I actually saw. The flames devouring a car are yellow and ravenous. It burns like a meteor. The fireball is destroying all traces of evidence of the body. Now no one will ever know. No one but four loyal friends. And me, Joanna Rigsby.

I turned off Penn's radio with a sharp snap of my wrist. "Do you think things you just hear about can be more real than things you actually experience?"

Penn's eyebrows lifted. "Is this a loaded question?"

"Not really." I shrugged.

Penn must have known I was thinking of Laurie Jenkins's death, but he didn't let on. It was better if we didn't talk about it. I knew that. I only wished I could quit thinking about it and could get rid of my nightmares. Ahead, a gap in the trees marked the turnoff to the cabin. When Penn turned into the dirt driveway, I saw that we were the last of the group to arrive. Two cars were out front, and our friends were sitting on the steps, waiting for us. On the top step was Casey MacNamara. He was pale, as was fitting to a computer geek. With his white face and thatch of carroty hair, he was a regular fixture at the school's computer lab, which he ran like his private kingdom. On the bottom step, side by side, sat Tessa West and Stephen Garner, looking amazingly alike. I wondered sometimes if that was why they felt such a strong attraction to each other. Wasn't there a Greek myth about a guy who fell in love with his own reflection? That story could have been about Stephen and Tessa. Their baggy clothes gave them each a sagging, street-person look, but a close glance showed that they were startlingly attractive in precisely the same way—untidy dark hair, damp, brilliant eyes, and carefully modeled chins and noses.

Penn got out of the car. "I thought I told you we were going to be late," he said apologetically.

"Joanna is still trying to shake off the flu."

"I needed to sleep in," I added.

"You could have given us a key," Casey snapped. "We could have gone in and lit a fire instead of freezing our butts off out here."

Penn ignored Casey's remark and began unloading the trunk. He loved this house in the woods; his parents had built it by hand back in the days when they were happily married. The place was full of good memories. No way was Penn going to give Casey a key.

Penn unlocked the door and pushed it open. Stepping inside, I felt a rush of happiness that almost took my breath away. Light spilled in the windows; the living room was almost entirely enclosed by glass. A pool of yellow sunshine warmed the wood floor in front of the window. The floor was bleached a lighter shade where the light fell. Slanting shafts of sun picked out floating specks of dust and set ablaze the copper bottoms of the pans hanging in the kitchen. A river ran behind the house, and beyond that, tall green pines and maples showed the first reddish bud of leaves.

Well-thumbed books filled the small bookcase beside the fireplace. Fat roses decorated the chintz on the sofa and chairs, and a pack of cards lay facedown on the low table in front of the couch.

I hoped this weekend was going to be easier than the last one. Then, Casey had brought a

portable record player and had insisted on playing
an annoying French song over and over. It grated
on everyone's nerves, and Penn had had to re-
strain Stephen from attacking Casey at one point.

I let my bag fall against the back of the sofa and
dropped onto the soft cushions, my nose pressed
against a chintz rose. I could hear chatter and the
opening and closing of the front door as the others
carried things in from their cars. Tessa laid a physics
book on the low table beside me. I involuntarily
winced. If it hadn't been for Stephen and Tessa's ef-
forts, I would have been flunking physics. As it was,
I was barely scraping by, and missing three days
with the flu was not going to help.

"My record!" screeched Casey. "How'd it end
up over there?" I propped myself up awkwardly
on my elbows. A record cover rested against the
big northern window. On it was a picture of a
French cabaret singer sketched in purple and
black. It was the record Casey had played endlessly. "Damn," said Casey, snatching it up.
"With the sun coming in on it like that, it could
have gotten warped."

Tessa's and Stephen's eyes met briefly, and I
knew suddenly that it was no accident the record
had been left leaning against the sunny window.
"It'll be all right," said Stephen coolly. "It's not
like you left it in the car or anything."

Casey slid the record out of its jacket and put

it on the record player. "It looks wavy!" he mourned. "I'll bet it's ruined."

The singer's voice rang out in a wavering parody of itself.

Casey snatched the needle off the record with an angry scratching sound. "Who put my record by the window?" he demanded. "It wasn't me."

Penn shrugged. "You remember how we were all rushing around when we left last time. Anybody could have stuck it there to get it out of the way."

"You guys did it on purpose," yelled Casey. "You were all complaining about the record. I guess you decided to do something about it, didn't you? Didn't you?"

"Don't be paranoid, Casey," said Tessa. "If we wanted to get rid of your record, it would have been easier just to step on it."

If I hadn't seen that quick glance between Tessa and Stephen, I might have thought she was telling the truth.

"Tell you what," said Penn. "I'll pay you for the record. Fair enough?"

"That record is valuable," Casey muttered. "It's a collector's item. It'll probably cost me fifty bucks to get another one."

We all knew he had found the old record in his family's garage. Penn, his face wooden, peeled two twenties and a ten off a stack of bills and laid them on Casey's open palm. Then he took the record off the phonograph, dropped it on the floor, and stepped on it. I heard the plastic crack.

"Hey, why'd you do that?" Casey cried.

"You said yourself it was ruined," said Penn.

"Yeah, but it had sentimental value!"

"You've got the record jacket to remember it by," said Penn, turning away.

After that the weekend fell into its familiar pattern. Tessa, as usual, got projects going. There were fires to build, games to play, fancy food to prepare. Tessa never liked to sit still for long. Stephen had brought a gun he'd found in a trunk in his family's attic, and for a while we tried target practice against an old outhouse. Stephen drew three concentric circles on its door with a Magic Marker and made cross-hatched lines on the smallest circle to indicate the bull's-eye. I hated the noise of the gun, and when my turn came, I squeezed my eyes shut as I pulled the trigger. The pistol leapt in my hands, and there was an explosion that made my ears ring painfully.

"Stop her," cried Casey. "She's a menace."

When I opened my eyes, I was embarrassed to see that my bullet had missed the outhouse altogether and put a round black hole in a pine tree five feet to its left. Blushing hotly, I handed the gun to Stephen. I watched, humbled, as he hit one bull's-eye after another.

We took walks in the woods. The first hint of unfolding leaves had appeared overhead on the bare branches, and sun glittered on the river, throwing odd moving patterns against the tree trunks. The moss smelled damp. I fell behind the others, too tired to keep pace, and Penn stayed with me. We sat on a damp fallen tree trunk, and after a few minutes I felt the wet sinking into the seat of my jeans. He touched the corner of my mouth with his finger and smiled. Overcome with peace and contentment, I let my head fall against the hollow of his shoulder.

"I wish we could stay here forever," I said. He stroked my hair, and I listened to my breath whistling gently against his shirt. "I wish the rest of the world didn't even exist," I added.

"I wish a lot of things," he said.

Laurie. Neither of us could seem to stop thinking about Laurie.

Once I was rested, we walked back to the cabin. It was quiet without the others, and when we stepped over the threshold, I felt as if the house were asleep. It was so peaceful in the cabin, with the golden light spilling in the window.

I stretched out on the couch at once, thankful not to be walking.

Penn smiled and squeezed onto the couch next to me. There wasn't enough room for both of us to lie on it, and he had his hand on the floor to keep from falling off. "Ditch the back cushions," he said, "so we'll have more room." He bumped his head on the coffee table. "Ouch." He rubbed it.

"This isn't going to work," I said, laughing.

"Sure it will. It's nice and cozy." Penn grabbed at the table with one hand for balance and managed to land a kiss on my lips.

"You're going to fall off!" I protested.

We heard voices, and suddenly Penn fell off the couch. I sat bolt upright, and he hastily got up and sat down beside me.

Casey threw the door open.

"My, my, my," he said. "Looks as if you two could stand to comb your hair. What could you guys have been doing on the couch that would get your hair so messed up? Studying physics?"

"Anybody for lunch?" asked Tessa quickly. "Penn, why don't you wash the lettuce. Casey, I've got a treat for you."

"Chocolate mousse?" He perked up hopefully.

Casey's mean streak always caught me off balance, and it was surprisingly hard for me to laugh off his frequent teasing.

Later I fell asleep over my physics book, but I was pleasantly conscious of the bustle of activity around me. I can see Tessa now, if I close my eyes, leaping up from our quiet circle around the fire: "Let's play poker—deuces, one-eyed jacks, suicide kings, and the man with the ax are wild," she would call cheerfully. She loved to cook and was continually getting us to help with the food. We picked the meat out of walnuts, shelled peas, shucked corn.

I spent a lot of time writing in my diary. Once or twice I had caught the others staring at the open pages, trying to make sense of the jumbled letters. I think they looked on my diary as one of my eccentricities, like my habit of scraping whipped cream off of hot chocolate and picking the nuts out of brownies.

"I am happy," I wrote that weekend. As I stared at the jumbled letters on the page, they easily rearranged themselves in my mind into English.

> *How is it possible to be happy when I know so much is wrong? Maybe the reason I can be happy is that I didn't know Laurie. Even though I know her body is rotting somewhere, she seems unreal, like somebody I've read about in a magazine. It's only because her death is a threat to the people I care about that it frightens me.*
>
> *I keep thinking of Penn handing those bills to Casey. Penn was paying him for that awful record! I saw the way Casey's greedy eyes glittered as each bill came out of Penn's*

wallet. He's bound to think there's more where that came from. Can't Penn see how dangerous that is? Casey knows all about Laurie's death. What if he wants money for keeping his mouth shut about that? Next time, fifty dollars isn't going to be enough.